MW01166643

SECOND EDITION

A FUTURE
and a *Hope*

Stories of Spiritual Healing after Abortion

CYNTHIA JORDAN

A FUTURE AND A HOPE
STORIES OF SPIRITUAL HEALING AFTER ABORTION

iUniverse books may be ordered through booksellers or by contacting:

iUniverse
1663 Liberty Drive
Bloomington, IN 47403
www.iuniverse.com
844-349-9409

ISBN: 978-1-6632-1283-2 (sc)
ISBN: 978-1-6632-1313-6 (e)

Library of Congress Control Number: 2020922313

Print information available on the last page.

iUniverse rev. date: 12/09/2020

For James and Amy

INTRODUCTION

I thought my life would go on normally after abortion. I could have neither predicted nor imagined the ways in which my family and my future would be forever altered. The choice was mine; the consequences weren't. Multiply that by all the other people who thought the same thing about their own lives. What our culture is left with, besides the void of millions of children, are their left-behind parents, many of whom, as a result of their abortion choice, remain sick at heart and in a state of dysfunction for the rest of their lives.

A Future and a Hope provides a glimpse into postabortion life through the fictionalized account of women who sought healing after their abortions. The people are not real, but many of the situations are. It is a faith-based story because seeking forgiveness from the Creator who formed me and my unborn children was the only course of action that made sense to me during my own search for forgiveness and restoration. Even if you don't believe in a Creator, I am hopeful you will suspend your disbelief long enough to read this story.

My prayer is that, in addition to hurting women, and men, people unfamiliar with abortion will read this book and begin to understand the unspeakable destruction this procedures leaves in its wake.

For those of you who made an abortion decision due to rape or incest, my heart goes out to you. While the reasons for your choice were dictated by tragic circumstances, the consequences of your decision are probably not unlike the ones found in the following pages.

There are two groups to whom I owe my deepest appreciation for my own healing and subsequent desire to write this book: the pastors I heard speak about abortion in loving, grace-filled ways, who were not intimidated about telling the truth; and the many women who came before me who were bold enough to speak up about their own pain and to help other women with theirs. It is an unfortunate sisterhood but a sisterhood nonetheless, and we are available to help you too.

CHAPTER 1

Sin

Then, after desire has conceived, it
gives birth to sin; and sin, when it
is full-grown, brings forth death.
—James 1:15

Lisa—Fifteen Years Ago

"Will you marry me, Lisa?"

"Oh yes, Chuck," Lisa said as she broke into tears. "I love you. You are the best thing that has ever happened to me."

Lisa remembered the proposal and her words as if it had been yesterday. She knew Chuck was a good man. She had been attracted to him instantly. It hadn't been easy raising two children by herself after the divorce. She dated a few times, but they were either sex maniacs or still lived with their mothers. Chuck was calm and self-assured, not to mention drop-dead handsome. Her next-door neighbor Karen had introduced them. Chuck was a contractor working on her room addition. Lisa had seen the slim, tanned figure go in and out next door several times, but she assumed he was a family friend or a brother-in-law. One day she was in the driveway getting into her car when Chuck was leaving Karen's house. Karen spotted Lisa and walked Chuck over to introduce him. By that time, Lisa was already in the car buckling her seat belt.

"Lisa," Karen had called out in her singsong way, "I want you to meet someone."

Great, Lisa thought, *I have no makeup on, and I'm still in my sweats. Oh well, it doesn't matter. I'll never see this person again.*

"Lisa, meet Chuck Wagner. He's our contractor on the house, but we've known him for years. He's just like family."

"Hi, Chuck. Nice to meet you."

Karen hadn't been satisfied with a simple introduction and turned to Chuck. "Lisa's a single parent too. Her girls are both grown and gone. Isn't that right, Lisa?"

"Yes, Debbie just left for college, and Diane will graduate from college next spring."

"My kids are both gone too," Chuck said. "I guess I haven't gotten used to the silence yet. I must be suffering from empty-nest syndrome."

"I know what you mean," Lisa said.

"Sorry, we're keeping you from leaving. Nice to meet you too, Lisa," Chuck said as he waved and backed away from the car.

Karen was still talking, but Lisa backed out of the driveway. Chuck was polite and seemed nice. He was definitely good-looking. He must have been about six feet two, and he had broad shoulders and a slim waist. No beer gut on this guy. There was graying around the temples, but he still had a full head of curly hair that fell to his collar. Based on the age of Chuck's kids and the laugh lines around his slate-blue eyes, Lisa judged him to be at least forty-five, maybe a little older. She looked at herself in the rearview mirror and wished she had made time for that makeup.

A couple of days later, her phone rang. "Hello, Lisa?"

"Yes," she answered to the man's deep voice.

"Uh, this is Chuck. From the other day. Do you remember?"

"Of course," she said. She hoped he couldn't tell by her voice how surprised she was to hear from him.

He continued, "Your neighbor is having a cookout on Saturday, and she has invited me. I was wondering if you would like to join us. It will just be Karen and Mark, Karen's parents, and me."

While Chuck talked, Lisa paced nervously. She suddenly tripped on the leg of the dining room table, and as she reached forward to break her fall, her phone went flying.

"Chuck? Are you still there?" Lisa asked as she hurriedly grabbed the phone and put it back to her ear.

"Yes, Lisa, I'm here."

"Why sure, I'd love to come," she said. "What can I bring?"

"Uh, I don't know. I can check with Karen and get back to you."

"No, that's okay. I'll call her," Lisa said.

On Saturday, Lisa tried not to get too excited about seeing Chuck again. *It's just a cookout,* she told herself. After she prepared a broccoli salad to take, she did some housework and showered. Unlike the other day when she had met Chuck, she took to time to carefully apply her makeup. Next, she dressed in white slacks that flattered her slim figure and chose a chocolate-brown tunic top. All eyes were on her when she crossed the lawn and arrived at her neighbor's cookout, especially Chuck's.

The cookout was wonderful. Chuck had a great sense of humor, and Lisa laughed louder than anyone else at his stories. He had a macho, man's man quality about him, and she was caught unawares by the effect he had on her. Just being near him physically was exciting. At the end of the evening, he came over to her, took both of her hands in his, leaned over, and kissed her on the cheek.

"This was fun, Lisa. I hope we can see each other again."

The wedding was eight months later. It had been a wonderful celebration with supportive family members on both sides. Lisa's two girls and Chuck's daughter, Sandy, were bridesmaids. His son, Harry, served as his dad's best man. Chuck's business partner and brother were the other groomsmen.

The honeymoon was a quick trip to the Great Smoky Mountains so Chuck could get back in time for the spring building season. Prior to the trip, Lisa had talked to her doctor and they agreed she was too old to go back on the pill. Lisa and Chuck were both raised in the Catholic Church and were familiar with how the rhythm method of birth control was *supposed* to work.

After six weeks of marriage, Lisa felt ill and realized she had missed her period. At first, she chalked it up to excitement about the wedding, but her symptoms persisted. To reassure herself she wasn't pregnant, she stopped at a drugstore for an at-home pregnancy test.

Lisa looked around the store to make sure she didn't see anyone she recognized. At the checkout counter, she fidgeted as the cashier eyed her purchase. The second time the cashier looked at Lisa and then down at the box, Lisa lied and said, "It's for my daughter."

"There's nothing like grandchildren," the woman said. "I hope it's positive."

Lisa could think of nothing else to say. She paid her bill and ran to her car where she burst into tears. *This can't be happening. It will be okay,* she told herself. *I'll get the test out of the way, and life will go on.*

Chuck had left work early to surprise Lisa by taking her out to dinner. He was waiting on her when she got home.

"Have you been crying?" he asked. "What's wrong?"

Lisa tried to speak, but all she could do was shake her head. She pointed to the bathroom as she ran in that direction.

"Are you sick?" Chuck yelled.

There was no response from Lisa until she came out of the bathroom a few minutes later holding up a piece of white plastic for Chuck to look at.

"What's that?" he asked.

"It's a pregnancy test. See the pink line?"

Chuck looked confused.

"Yeah."

"We're pregnant."

Chuck stared at her. "What? We're too damned old to start over with kids now. We had enough problems raising the ones we've got. There's a way to take care of this, Lisa."

A jolt of rejection hit Lisa like a burst of winter wind. "You mean an abortion?"

Chuck sighed. "Yeah, I think that would be the best thing. Don't you?"

She knew he didn't want to hear what she really thought, and she knew that in order to keep her new husband happy, she would have the abortion. There was no other choice.

"I suppose you're right," she said.

"Good. Now, let's go get a bite to eat."

"Not tonight, Chuck. You go."

Lisa closed the bedroom door behind her. Hours later, she heard him come to bed, but she pretended to be asleep. The next morning, Lisa made breakfast, and she and Chuck ate in silence. After he left for work, Lisa made the appointment. When the day came, she went by herself and paid for it by herself. Chuck never mentioned it again.

Lisa buried the memories of the experience. Two years later, at age forty-one, she was pregnant again. This time, she didn't tell Chuck.

As she lay on the table in the recovery room, she remembered the last time she had gotten pregnant. This time, the decision had been much easier. Two babies gone. She must be an awful person, but Chuck had been right the first time. They were too old to start another family.

Donna—Ten Years Ago

Wait until Dad's congregation hears the pastor's daughter is pregnant and doesn't even know who the father is. Donna laughed and laughed. Then she cried. *It doesn't matter,* she thought to herself. *Dad is never going to know.*

She went to the campus medical center and got a referral to an abortion clinic. In her second year of nursing school, no one had to tell Donna it was really a baby. She didn't want to acknowledge the fact, but she also knew it wasn't just a blob of tissue or "undifferentiated cells," as the young girl in the clinic told her. *"Who do they think they're kidding?"* she asked herself.

Donna thought about her lifestyle and how she had changed since going away to college. She didn't enjoy everything she was involved in, but she couldn't help trying everything either. On several occasions, she vowed to herself to change her drinking habits and her pattern of dating several men at the same time, but things didn't change. She knew she wasn't great looking, and she certainly wasn't wealthy, but she had a good figure, and she liked to party. She considered her uninhibited enjoyment of men and of sex her best feature.

Growing up in her home had been all about inhibitions. Don't do this, don't do that. She had known Christians in her church who seemed happy and joyful, but she didn't know how to be that way herself. A newcomer to her loose-knit group of friends had interested her. Gary was six feet tall, had beautiful, curly blond hair, and was more reserved than the rest. Some of her friends joked that he was cerebral. She liked that he wanted to talk about art, music, and current affairs, but she was annoyed when he didn't want to be intimate on their first date. In a few weeks, he changed his mind and had since made up for lost time. She considered him one of her favorites. She hadn't counted on his reaction when she casually mentioned her period was late.

"You think you're pregnant? That's great! Let's get married," he said.

"Oh yeah, that's just what I want to do," she said.

"I'm serious! I would love to be married to you, and I would love to have a baby. This may not be ideal timing, but let's go for it. We can look at rings later this week. Then we'll tell our families and start planning a wedding."

"I can't marry you," she said.

"Why not? We're good together. What are you afraid of?"

"I don't want to be married, and I certainly don't want to have a child."

"Donna, that's my child too."

She wasn't positive the child was his. There had been a weekend when Gary was out of town, and she had run into an old friend. A close friend.

"Are you sure?" she asked him. She hated the hurt look on his face.

"Get out," she screamed. "You have nothing to say about it."

Gary studied her for a moment, then said calmly, "I get it. It's overwhelming news, but it's also exciting. We can work through this, Donna. I promise. Get some rest. I'll call you tomorrow."

Gary sounded upbeat in his first voice mail. "Hey,

sweetie. Hope you're feeling okay. Everything happens for a reason, and this will be a new beginning for us. Call me. I'd like to come over after work. Love you."

Donna didn't call Gary back and camped out at a friend's for almost two weeks so he couldn't catch her at home. His subsequent voice mails became more urgent and, to Donna, more annoying. She didn't return to her apartment until after her clinic appointment. That day, she answered the phone when he called.

"Donna, why haven't you called me back? Where have you been?" Gary asked.

"Today, I was at the abortion clinic. It's over, Gary. There's no more baby, and there's not going to be a wedding."

"Please tell me you're kidding. You can't be serious. I love you. I love our child."

"Gary, stop. We both knew this wasn't going to work."

"You're wrong, Donna. It could have worked. Did you really do this thing?"

"Yes, Gary."

"Well, are you okay?"

Donna could hear the tremble in Gary's voice. She couldn't wait to have the abortion, and now she couldn't wait to get rid of Gary.

"I'm fine. Just leave me alone."

"I'm coming over," Gary said.

"No, Gary. I don't want to see you. We were a mistake from the start. Find someone who cares about you."

"But you care about me, and I care about you," Gary said. "How could you do this to us?"

"There is no us, Gary. Don't come over here. I don't

want to see you. I'm hanging up now and please don't call anymore."

Donna heard from mutual friends about how broken up Gary was over losing her and the baby. She already knew. His number came up on her phone several times a day. She never picked up, but he always left a voice mail, which she never listened to. It took four months for him to give up.

Tanika—Seventeen Years Ago

Tanika and her friend Jodie were walking home together, talking excitedly about the end of their freshman year and the upcoming summer break.

"Do you think you'll get that perfect attendance award again this year, Tanika?"

"Only three more weeks to go. Hope so. I already know I have you beat!"

"Shoot, I don't know how you go all year and not miss. What are you going to do this summer?"

"I'm going to volunteer at the rec center."

"Volunteer?"

"We're too young to get paid, but the director said if I do a good job, he'll hire me as a counselor next summer. Why don't you come with me, Jodie? They need more people."

"Not me. I'm going to the pool every day."

"Are you joining the swim team?"

"Why would I want to do that? They practice at like eight in the morning."

"I didn't think so. You're just going to that pool to meet guys. Like they care about you."

"That's not true, Tanika. Since we started wearing makeup and going to Mrs. Johnson for our hair, I see lots of guys checking us out."

"So? That's what guys do. It don't mean nothing. When you get tired of the pool, come on over to the rec center."

"No thanks, but when you get tired of all that volunteering, you can hang out with me. See you tomorrow," Jodie said as she turned to walk toward her house.

"See ya."

As Tanika continued down the block, a boy she recognized from the neighborhood came up beside her. "Girl, you look fine. Are you gonna be with me?"

"Get outta here, Dwayne. Why would I wanna do that?"

"I'll be good to you, Tanika."

"Yeah, that's what you say to all the girls."

"Are you still just a girl, or are you a woman?"

"Dwayne, you're bad. Leave me alone."

"I can make you a woman, Tanika. You'll like it." Dwayne leaned in to give Tanika a kiss. When she tried to move away, Dwayne grabbed her by the arms.

"Dwayne, lemme go. I'll scream, so help me."

"Shh. I didn't mean nothin'," Dwayne said as he released her and backed away. "I just wanted a little kiss. You're so pretty, Tanika. Just gimme a little kiss. Then I'll leave you alone. I bet you've never been kissed before."

Tanika giggled.

"See, girl. You was just waitin' for me to come along. How 'bout that kiss? I'm not begging. Either you want to kiss me or you don't."

Dwayne was handsome and very persuasive. No one had ever asked her for a kiss before. She felt a strange, exciting tingle all over her body.

"Okay, Dwayne," she said. "Just one little kiss."

Tanika closed her eyes and tilted her head toward Dwayne's face. Dwayne picked her up and dragged her away from the sidewalk. He knocked her to the ground under a huge tree behind the nearest house. As soon as she was on the ground, Tanika started to scream. He slapped her hard. Then he placed his mouth over hers and lay on top of her. No one could hear her moans and muffled screams. Dwayne tore the button from Tanika's slacks and quickly pulled them down. With a burst of pain, Dwayne pushed his way inside her. Everything happened so quickly. When he rolled off of her, he got up and ran away. Tanika lay there silently. She thought about screaming, but she didn't want anyone to see her like that. She straightened her clothes, retrieved her spilled purse and books, and went home. She unlocked the door, paused to make sure no one was there, and ran upstairs. She hid her bloody underwear and grass-stained slacks in the back of her closet. She got in the shower and sobbed. *No one will ever know*, she said to herself.

Tanika saw Dwayne after that, but he ignored her.

"Girl, you better not a-gone and gotten yourself pregnant," the woman shouted at her.

"Auntie Jo, I don't know what you mean!" Tanika cried.

"You know exactly what I mean, you little bitch."

The old woman sprang at the girl and slapped her across the face.

"You ain't had a period in two months. Don't you dare lie to me, Tannie."

"I didn't mean to," Tanika said. "It just happened."

"Yeah, it just happened. I'm gonna git you outta this mess, and it had better never 'just happen' again, or you on the street."

"Auntie Jo, what do you mean? I want this baby," Tanika said.

"Shoot. You nothing but a baby yourself. You got no business having a baby. Don't I got enough trouble raisin' you and that no-good brother of yours?"

"But, Auntie Jo, maybe Aunt Lou could keep the baby until I finish school," Tanika said.

"Lou? Tannie, you think straight for once. Lou already got two babies, and you got three more years of school. I say I will take care of this, and I will."

"Auntie Jo," Tanika sobbed, "I want my baby."

"You hush, girl. Go to bed."

Tanika cried herself to sleep. The next morning, she begged her great-aunt to let her have her baby, but the old woman wouldn't budge. A few days later in school, Tanika was called to the office at the beginning of fourth period.

"Tanika, your great-aunt is here to pick you up for your doctor's appointment," the secretary said. "Aren't you feeling well?"

"What?" Tanika asked

"C'mon, Tannie. We don't want to be late," the girl's great-aunt said.

The woman guided her out of the office before there was any more conversation.

"Auntie Jo, please don't make me do this. Please. Please!"

"Get in the car, Tannie."

The woman drove in silence as Tanika sobbed. At the clinic, the nurse told the old woman the teenager had to stop crying before they would take her in. Tanika heard and looked into her great-aunt's eyes. She stopped crying.

Meredith—Three Months Ago

She felt the baby drop into the toilet. Thank God it was over. The past two days had been hell. Once she swallowed the medicine to weaken her cervix, she immediately had second thoughts, but there was no turning back. Twenty-four hours later, she took the next dose of medicine to begin her contractions.

It's better this way, she told herself. *Now I can concentrate on my career.* She thought about the night she ran into John, a guy who had been in one of her law school classes.

"Hi, Meredith. Looks like you're celebrating."

"You bet, Johnny boy," was her too-loud, too-drunk response. "I just landed a job at the firm of Palmer, Palmer & Ernst," she said, with special emphasis on the Ps.

"Congratulations, Meredith! May I buy you a drink?"

"Sure, Johnny. Join us. My table is over there." Meredith pointed with a flourish.

The next thing Meredith remembered was waking up in her apartment with John on the other side of her bed. *For Chrissake*, she thought, *I can't even remember his last name.*

"Get up and get out," she shouted.

"That's not what you said last night," John said as he sat up in bed. "As a matter of fact, you were quite the hostess."

"You creep, you knew I was drunk."

"Did not."

"How did we get here?"

"Don't worry. I drove you."

"Then you must have known I was in no shape to drive. Take me back so I can get my car."

They dressed and drove in silence until John pulled up by Meredith's car.

"Here you are. Congrats on the job, Meredith. I'll call you."

"Don't bother."

Meredith got out and slammed the door, relieved to be rid of her former classmate. She had two weeks until she started her new job, and she didn't have time to get involved with John or anyone else. She spent most of the time reading, but went shopping once with her mother for new work clothes. She had to be ready mentally and appearance-wise to make a good impression.

Life became a whirlwind. There was so much to learn about the law and about working at a firm. She expected long hours, and she was not disappointed. She ran on little sleep and even less food. It was another three or four weeks before she realized her period was late. She couldn't believe she might be pregnant. No way would she let a slipup ruin her career. She had worked too long and too hard to get where she was. She arranged for extra time at lunch and went to Planned Parenthood. There they confirmed her pregnancy and suggested RU-486 as a very private, effective way to solve her problem.

They had been right. She scheduled the procedure so she expelled the "tissue" over the weekend and returned to work on Monday morning. No one would be any the wiser.

Natalie—Seven Years Ago

"What do you want to do?" she asked him.

"Have the abortion, of course," he answered.

She felt a sudden void in the pit of her stomach. "I just thought …"

"You thought? What did you think?" he asked mockingly. "Did you think about how you just landed a starting position on a Big Ten basketball team? Have you thought about what will happen to your scholarship?"

"I want to talk this through, Ned," she said. The firm tone of her voice surprised her.

"There's nothing to talk about. I have medical boards in three weeks. I don't have time for this. Just take care of it."

"It?"

"You know what I mean."

"Abortions are expensive. I don't have any money. I can't put it on my insurance for my parents to see."

"I'll help you. Gotta go."

She was shocked at Ned's reaction. She wanted the fairy tale. She believed it was possible for them to be married and have the baby while Ned went to medical school. She would go to classes in the evenings or online to get her degree and still have time for a family. Her basketball career paled in comparison to a child. *He will change his mind*, she told herself.

She remembered the day she met Ned. It was only two weeks after she arrived on campus, the first time she had ever been away from home. He was sitting with her roommate in the library. She noticed he was cute and looked older than other freshmen.

"Hey, Natalie, this is Ned. He's my biology tutor."

"Hi, Ned."

He asked politely where she was from and what she was studying. The three of them made small talk for a few minutes until her roommate apologized and said she really needed to get back to her studies. Natalie excused herself but glanced back at the friendly biology scholar.

Ned asked the roommate for Natalie's number and called her the following week. She was thrilled. Their first date had been to meet at McDonald's after their classes. He razzed her about her choice of salad with no dressing and bottled water, but he seemed very interested in her physical training and her muscular build.

"You must spend hours in the gym and on the court, and I hear you're an excellent student. I appreciate the discipline it takes."

"How old are you?" she had blurted out, anxious to take the attention away from herself.

"I'm twenty-two," he said. "I graduate in the spring, then medical school."

"That takes discipline too," she remembered saying to him.

She also remembered that on their first date, she

decided there was something different about him. Stability. That was it. Ned was older, disciplined, and self-assured. She decided on the spot he was much cooler than the guys she dated in high school. She hadn't planned to get involved with anyone so soon, but she did. She and Ned became inseparable.

With shaking hands, Natalie got online and searched under "abortion." Five days later, she sat alone in an office at a place called Gentle Care Clinic. The "procedure," as they called it, had taken longer than they said it would, and it had been excruciatingly painful. She couldn't even remember the doctor's name. After it was over, he said that in six short weeks she could "go out and party again." Was that supposed to be some kind of joke?

The nurse led Natalie to a row of recliners where five or six other ladies were bundled up in blankets, left to their own thoughts. The nurse covered Natalie as soon as she sat down and offered her juice and crackers. Natalie declined. *Isn't that what they give kids in Sunday school?* she asked herself. She shivered under the blanket from the pain and the shock of what she had done. She tried to shake off the noises she had heard and the permeating smell of disinfectant. She wanted to get the hell out of there.

"You look a little pale," the nurse said when she came back to check on her. "Why don't you rest a while longer. Is someone waiting on you?"

"No, but I'm okay to drive," Natalie lied. "I'd like to get my clothes now."

The nurse didn't protest and led her to a dressing room.

The pain and the smell stayed with Natalie as she walked out the door and headed to the bus stop. She wished she had asked someone to drive her, but no one knew about this except Ned, and he was busy.

Once home, she called him. He finally answered on the fifth ring.

"Oh, hi, how are you?" he asked.

"I'm okay," she said. "It was four hundred dollars."

"What? Oh yeah. I'll send you a check."

"Ned, could you come over for a while?"

"Not tonight, Natalie. I'm studying. Don't you have someone else you can talk to?"

"Sure, Ned. Good night."

There had followed an awkward series of phone calls during which Natalie yelled, screamed, and cried. Ned wanted to avoid a face-to-face encounter with her but wanted to get the stuff he had left in her room. He went there when he knew Natalie would be in class and her roommate could let him in. When Natalie came home, she was excited to see his writing on an envelope addressed to her that had been left on her desk. She tore it open, hoping for a letter expressing his love for her, or at least an apology. Inside was a check for $200 for his half of the abortion.

Natalie never saw Ned again.

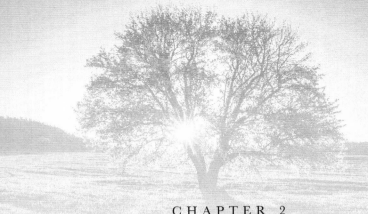

CHAPTER 2

A New Beginning

I will repay you for the years
the locusts have eaten.
—Joel 2:25

Group—Week One

Natalie was late. She pulled into the parking lot of the three-story redbrick building, ran for the entrance, and didn't breathe until she pushed the elevator button for the third floor. She tapped her foot during the slow ride up, then raced down the hallway until she found the door marked Conference Room. There she paused. *This was a mistake. I'll call them tomorrow and make some excuse.*

The door opened widely. "Natalie! So good to see you. Come join us. We're just getting started."

Natalie quietly followed the older woman into the

room. Several other ladies were already seated at a large, rectangular table. Natalie folded her five feet, eleven inch frame into a chair next to a young, petite woman, then picked up the blank name tag at her place and filled it out.

She recognized two of the women—the one who retrieved her from the hallway and the other volunteer leader. She had met with them three weeks ago when she came to learn about this workshop. They were also "postabortal," as they called it, and now volunteered to lead groups like this.

The older one reminded her of her aunt Edie. June was sixty-something, short, and heavy, just like her aunt, and her eyes and smile had the same wise look. The biggest difference was that June had quit coloring her hair, and now her blunt cut was tricolor, from the roots out. Aunt Edie would never allow a gray hair to be seen in the light of day. The other lady, Sofia, was maybe five or six years older than she was. Sofia was of average height, slim, and had shoulder-length black hair. Her coloring and dark eyes suggested Hispanic descent.

"Welcome, ladies," June said. "It's good to see each of you again. Let's get started. First, thank you for coming. It takes a great deal of courage to come forward and deal with this issue. Tonight is the beginning of a very difficult but rewarding journey. Sofia, would you lead us in prayer?"

"Okay," Sofia responded quietly. "Lord, we love you and thank you for these women who are here this evening. We turn this time over to you. We ask that each woman feels safe here tonight and that each will see your hand in the material we cover. Bless this time, we pray, in Jesus's name. Amen."

"Everyone, grab a pen," June said. "If you're right-handed, place the pen in your left hand. If you're left-handed, put the pen in your right hand. Ready? Now, turn to the first page of your manual and write your name with the wrong hand."

Natalie couldn't imagine why. "The wrong hand?" she asked.

"Yes," June answered. "If you're right-handed, use your left, and vice versa."

Natalie thought it was a silly thing to do, but she, along with the others, completed the exercise.

In a few minutes, June asked them how they did.

The women laughed. "It feels really strange," one of them called out.

"Of course, it does." June smiled. "The purpose of this exercise is to give you an idea of how strange you're going to feel in this group for a while. You're going to be able to speak openly about your abortion, and that will be a first for most of you. Everything we do and say here will be different from what you've experienced since the time of your abortions. We will talk about things you've kept hidden, and we will look at ourselves in new ways. It will be a difficult but life-changing journey."

Natalie studied the shaky scrawl of her name. *That's definitely different,* she thought.

"Let's move on. Now we're going to break into pairs. We don't have an even number of participants, so Meredith, you pair up with Sofia. What we want you to do is use a word picture to describe to your partner how you feel about your abortion. For example, some people may say they feel stretched like a rubber band. Maybe you

22

feel like a ball, bouncing from one emotion to another. Use your imagination to describe your feelings. Then you're going to come back to the group and introduce your partner using the word picture they used to describe themselves. Any questions? If not, take about ten minutes to come up with your word pictures."

The thought of having to describe her feelings made Natalie break out in a cold sweat. While she was still thinking about what June had asked them to do, the woman next to her said, "Hi, I'm Donna. Do you want to pair up?" Natalie smiled and nodded.

"I'll go first," Donna said. "I can't believe I'm doing this. Let's see ... I guess I'm a hot-air balloon. I'm soaring overhead and seeing my life from the outside. The peaks, the valleys. My life is actually pretty good right now, but I keep looking back over my shoulder and seeing the valleys. It's like I can't leave them behind. How about you?"

Natalie was fascinated by how fast Donna talked. She was probably in her late thirties or early forties, but her animated speech and habit of punching the air as she made a point made her seem like a teenager. Her ease in describing herself gave Natalie the courage to plunge in.

"I'm not a hot-air balloon, but I feel like a regular balloon that's just about to burst. The pressure has been building and building, and my emotions are stretched to the limit. I feel like I'm going to explode if I don't deal with this issue in my life."

Natalie felt good saying it, but the look on her face must have concerned Donna. She reached over, took Natalie's hand in hers, and said, "Don't you worry. We're going to be okay."

"Oh, I'm not worried," Natalie lied, "but thank you."

Natalie and Donna were finished before anyone else. Natalie looked around the room to study faces and name tags. The girl named Tanika had moved her chair to work with Lisa, and Meredith was with Sophia. Natalie noticed how Lisa and Tanika chatted easily and were smiling, while Sophia had to pull out each word from a somber-faced Meredith.

After a few minutes, it was time for the women to introduce each other. Natalie and Donna went first. After that, it was difficult for Natalie to pay attention because she kept thinking maybe she shouldn't have come to the group. *I should have left things alone.* She didn't hear Lisa introduce Tanika as "a rudderless boat going in circles" or Tanika's introduction of Lisa as "a locked box." It was Sofia's introduction of Meredith that stirred her from her introspection.

"This is Meredith, and she described herself as 'a warm soda with all the fizz gone,'" Sophia said as Meredith looked at the floor.

It struck Natalie as odd. She thought Meredith's depression might be worse than her own.

Next, Sofia distributed a handout based on the findings of Teri and Paul Reisser. She explained that the Reissers, she a family therapist and he a psychiatrist, had become experts on something called "postabortion stress," based on their years of counseling postabortive women. *At least there's a name for what I'm feeling,* Natalie said to herself.

"As we can see from our exercise just now," Sofia said, "many of us have emotions that are wound tightly. Some of you have been experiencing emotions that you have never connected to your abortion. What we are going to learn is that many of these symptoms are of postabortion stress, or PAS for short. We're going to go over these now, and as I read through them, I want you to think about which ones apply to your life."

After Sophia briefly elaborated on each emotion on the lengthy list, she asked, "Can any of you relate to these symptoms?"

Natalie quickly reviewed the list in her mind. Guilt? Check. Anxiety? Check. Avoidance behaviors? Check. Then she stopped. *Good grief,* she thought. *I can relate to most of them.*

"Well, almost all of them," Lisa said. "I especially have trouble around Mother's Day. Both of my due dates would have been in May, and I have always dreaded that day. Don't get me wrong; it's nice to celebrate with my living children, but I always think about my two babies that are missing. I'm usually a first-class grump on Mother's Day. I guess I feel guilty celebrating it because I wasn't much of a mother to the two I destroyed."

Lisa grabbed a tissue from the box on the table and caught the tears running down her cheeks.

"It explains a lot about my drinking and drug use," Donna said. "I drank a lot and did drugs before the abortion, but it escalated afterward. I've been through rehab five times. The last time was just last year. I'm beginning to understand now why it has been so hard."

"I can relate to the bonding thing," Tanika said. "Sometimes I know I haven't been doing right by my kids. Almost like I didn't deserve to have them anyway, so I've kept them at arm's length. It's complicated. My great-aunt took me for my abortion, and later she helped me with my son and daughter and was closer to them than I was. When she died six months ago, I began to realize I didn't have much of a relationship with them. They're young yet, so I still have time, but I've lost the years when I wasn't there for them."

Natalie felt a mixture of empathy for the other women and disbelief that she could personally relate to so much of what had been said. The women glanced in her direction, indicating it was her turn to talk, but she had nothing to add. Neither did Meredith.

Sophia broke the silence. "Review this list," she said. "It is important to realize that many of our behaviors we have blamed on other things are actually a response to our abortions."

June began to talk as she produced a flip chart from the back of the room. "Before we move forward, let's make a list of things you plan to accomplish during our eight weeks together. Then, at the end of our workshop, you can see your progress and note the areas that still need work. While you write these things in your workbooks, I will record them up here. Call out whatever you want to deal with over the next several weeks. Natalie, would you like to go first?"

Natalie's throat went dry. She felt her ears get hot, which meant they were turning bright red. She was thankful her long hair covered them, or everyone would be able to see how nervous and embarrassed she was.

She finally heard herself say, "There are a lot of things I want to accomplish in this group. Most of all, I want to be able to forgive myself."

"Okay. Anything else?"

"Forgive myself and the baby's father."

June recorded Natalie's comments on the chart. "That's good. Tanika?"

Natalie sighed and turned her attention to Tanika.

"I just mentioned, my great-aunt was my guardian. I never knew my dad, and my mom died when I was two years old. Anyway, my great-aunt forced me to have the abortion. I know she meant to do what was best for me, but I still have bad feelings about the whole thing. I never forgave her. Now that she's gone, I've placed feeling guilty on top of my unforgiveness. I need to deal with all that."

Natalie couldn't imagine not knowing her parents or the thought of her own aunts encouraging her to have an abortion.

June nodded and wrote down "forgive great-aunt" and "stop feeling guilty."

"Donna?"

"I still feel so unhappy about my decision. I guess one thing I want to accomplish is to get rid of the sadness I feel. Also, at some point, I want to feel strong enough to talk to others about my experience, to help them know why they shouldn't choose abortion. I also feel like I owe the father of my baby an apology."

Natalie could immediately relate to the sadness part, but she didn't want to talk publicly to anyone about her experience. She knew she needed to forgive the baby's father, but an apology? It was she who deserved the apology, certainly not the other way around.

"Get rid of sadness, help others, ask for forgiveness,"

June repeated. "Lisa, what results are you looking for from this group?"

"Well, my second husband is the father of the babies. I'd like to be able to talk to him about it. The subject is a wall that's built up between us."

Uh-oh. Natalie thought about her husband and was overcome with feelings of guilt.

"We haven't heard from you, Meredith," June said.

"I guess I also need to forgive myself," Meredith answered in a low monotone.

Natalie listened as the others continued to contribute to the list until fifteen items were recorded on the flip chart.

"Let's take a ten-minute break," Sophia said. "There are cold drinks in the refrigerator and snacks on the counter. Please help yourselves. When we come back, June and I will briefly share our abortion experiences, and we'll ask you to do the same."

Natalie remembered talking to Sophia and June before the workshop about the importance of sharing during group, but she didn't think there would be so much sharing so soon. Memories of the day she had her abortion came rushing back. *I don't want to talk about this*, she thought to herself.

"C'mon, Natalie," Donna said, "let's get something to drink."

Natalie followed Donna to a large, adjoining kitchen with a table and several chairs. She grabbed a bottled water but wasn't enticed by the fresh fruit, pretzels, or brownies. She didn't feel like eating or socializing. She sat quietly, dreading the rest of the evening. Donna broke the awkward silence in the room by asking Lisa and Tanika about their families. Meredith remained standing at the counter, away from the rest of them. Donna asked her if she wanted to join them, but she responded with a curt "no thanks." After a few minutes of small talk, the ladies returned to the meeting room.

"As we mentioned earlier," June said, "Sofia and I will share our abortion experiences, and then you will have a chance to tell us something about yours. I'll go ahead and start. I had an abortion in college. I wasn't even sure who the father was. I didn't tell either of the men I was dating. It was my first time away from home, and I went a little crazy, but I was serious about my studies. Abortion seemed like my only option. I grew up in church and I knew deep down it was wrong, but I didn't want to mess up school, and I certainly didn't want my parents to find out."

Natalie could relate to the "crazy" part.

"As soon as it was over, I went on as if nothing had happened. Several years later, I met the man I married. By then, I was back in church, and I was honest with him from the beginning. Telling him I had made this decision earlier in life was one of the hardest things I have ever done. He's the kind of guy who always sees the best in people. He was wonderful about it, but I would be lying if I said it didn't affect our marriage. Once I told him, he never wanted to discuss it again.

"We started a family and had a comfortable lifestyle, yet I could never understand why I was so unhappy. Not only was I unhappy, I made everyone else in the family miserable with my nagging and nitpicking. My husband

and I had already been married with kids before I went through this group myself, more than twenty-five years ago. It wasn't until then that I realized what was going on with me and my behavior. The group by itself would have made a big difference in my life, but the fact that my husband came alongside me to help me through was huge. I remember feeling that this group gave me, my husband, and my kids a new beginning." June smiled. "Of course, I still have bad days, but now I recognize where those feelings are coming from, and I have the tools to deal with them."

Natalie wished June hadn't talked so much about her husband.

"As far as the actual abortion," June said, "I still remember the pain, and I'll always remember a very strange incident that happened. I had a woman doctor. When the procedure was over, she showed me the baby's feet. I was horrified."

Judging by the gasps around the room, so was everyone else.

"She did *what?*" Sophia asked.

"She held up the little feet so I could see them. I want to believe she didn't do it maliciously, but I'll never know. It was just the weirdest thing. Anyway, that will forever be my memory of my abortion and of my baby."

Natalie felt sick. She wondered why people are so cruel to each other. Then she wondered how she and this group of seemingly normal women could have been so cruel to their own children.

Sofia began her story. "I have had two abortions. One was when I was nineteen and in college. The father was my high school sweetheart. I didn't want to give up school, and I didn't want to tell my parents, so I had the abortion. Ironically, I was so messed up afterward that I dropped out of college for almost a year. The second abortion was when I was twenty-seven. Oh, I vowed I would never do it again, but I did. The decision was easier the second time. It's almost as if once you cross that line, once you have committed that sin and think of yourself as someone capable of doing such a thing, it's the first option you think of. I had just started a new job, the first real step in my career. As a single woman working with mostly men, I could only imagine the embarrassment and the effects it would have on my job. So, I had the abortion, and I ended up staying in that job for less than a year."

It was difficult to think about having two abortions. Natalie couldn't imagine going through it twice.

Sophia continued. "When I look back at things, I can see I sacrificed my children to the idols of education and career. I remember things being very hurried in the clinics. The pain was awful. I did not receive any type of counseling or information about other options. Emotionally, in both cases, it was a feeling of total rejection of me and of the baby."

Rejection. Natalie hated that word.

"Both men were ambivalent about whether or not I had their children, but the first man came to me many years later and apologized for his role in the abortion. That helped in my ability to forgive him. The other man was never sorry and said so. It's harder to forgive someone like that."

That's right, Natalie thought. *How am I supposed to think about forgiving Ned when he never even spoke to me again?* A few months after her abortion, she found out from a classmate that he had passed his exams and was accepted to medical school in another state. One time, she looked him up on the internet. She thought about calling or writing him, but for what purpose?

"I first went through a postabortion program at my church two years ago," Sofia said. "I'll never forget it. There were three of us, and I was the only one who cried. Can you believe it? So, if any of you is a crier, you have company! Anyway, both of the other women had been in counseling, and I guess they had cried all their tears. The thing I remember most is that one of the women had been addicted to speed and experienced seven abortions, all by her own hand. It was an awful thing to hear about, just like June's story about her baby's feet. It's important to realize that in the weeks ahead, you may hear things far better or worse than your own experience, but this group is not about judging each other. We have all sinned and fallen short of the glory of God. We want you to feel free to share your experience, no matter what it involved. That's why we talked with each of you when we first met you about the importance of confidentiality and making this group a safe place for sharing."

Seven abortions? The baby's feet? Natalie was already hearing things she considered horrific. *Is the entire workshop going to be like this?*

"Thank you, Sophia," June said. "Who would like to go next?"

The women looked at one another. Sofia and June

shared a glance, and June said, "Natalie, are you ready to share?"

I'll never be ready, Natalie thought, but she started talking. She hated the way her voice quivered, but she kept going. She tried to hold her head up, but her eyes locked on her hands on the table in front of her. As she talked, her fingers clenched and unclenched as if she had no control over them. She recounted her affair with Ned and how shattered she had been by his reaction to their pregnancy.

"I couldn't believe he wouldn't go with me to the clinic. I felt so alone. And the procedure? I've tried to wipe it out of my mind, but the smell of disinfectant still takes me back to that dark, cold room."

As she shared her story, in her mind's eye, she could see Ned scowling at her for divulging their secret.

"I continued to play basketball," she said, "but nothing was the same after the abortion. I felt hurt and abandoned. I lost my focus. At one time, my dream was to become an All American and be drafted into the WNBA, but my dreams never materialized. I became a phys ed teacher and married the first person who asked me. I've never told my husband about the abortion. He thinks I'm playing pickleball tonight. Only recently have I reflected on the price I paid, and continue to pay, for my abortion. I know now it has affected every area of my life. And along the way, we found out my doctor doesn't think we are able to get pregnant. That news made me bury the pain even deeper. I heard someone speak about abortion rights on TV the other night, and I was afraid I might put my fist through the screen. It isn't about women's rights; it's about people's lives. Anyway, I heard someone at church mention this program, and I knew it was time to do something about these feelings I've kept to myself all this time."

She suddenly gulped for air when the sobs she had held back for so long shook her body.

The other participants looked concerned, and Donna started to get up to go to Natalie's side.

"Let's all stay seated," June said gently. "We will be quiet and give Natalie the time she needs. You are among friends here, Natalie," June whispered. "Just let it out."

Once Natalie's uncontrollable sobs abated, her breathing returned to normal. When she looked up, she saw Tanika across the table smiling a sympathetic smile.

"It's okay," Tanika reassured her. "We've all been where you are." Natalie nodded and smiled.

"Thank you for sharing, Natalie," June said. "Please don't be embarrassed about crying. What you just did—sharing about your abortion—is one of the hardest things you will ever do."

June asked Lisa if she would like to go next. Lisa had a petite figure, but deep laugh lines around her eyes and graying hair around her face made her look every bit of fifty-something. Yet Natalie saw a youthful quality to her ready smile and bright blue eyes.

Lisa beamed when she talked about her courtship with Chuck.

"Well, he's so nice and so handsome," she said. "I hoped from the very start that we would get together. I agreed with him that we were too old to start a family. At least I let him talk me into that way of thinking. I couldn't believe my luck in finding him in middle age, and I didn't want to cross him. I didn't want to rock the boat. He's a great guy, but he's totally oblivious to what this has done to me—to us.

"At church several months ago, I found myself telling a women's group about my abortions. I knew that if God gave me the strength to talk about it, that it was time for me to deal with this more deeply. Chuck and I have been part of a church family for almost three years now. We've heard our pastor preach about abortion several times, and I know Chuck thinks about what happened, but we've never dealt with it together. At this point in my life, I am so sad about what I did and so full of regret. Our babies would be teenagers by now. I miss what never will be, what we will never have."

Lisa's voice trailed off. Natalie began to realize that everyone's story was a story about rejection and loss. Every story was about living apart from God.

"Tanika, will you go next?" June asked.

"Yes, ma'am," Tanika replied. "I'm thirty-two years old and the single mother of two kids. They are great. Their dad sees them often and pays child support on time every month. I have a decent job, and last year, after lots of hard work, I got my degree. So, what's the problem? Lately, all I can think about is the baby I aborted when I was fifteen. I was raped. Then, as I mentioned earlier, my great-aunt forced me to have the abortion. Afterward, it was never mentioned again. Not the rape and not the abortion. Since she died, the bitterness and anger I have felt toward her all this time started coming to the surface. I know I didn't have a choice because I lived with her and didn't have any other place to go. I was powerless. I know she did what she thought was best for me, but I begged her not to take me for the abortion. I knew it was wrong. In January, on the anniversary of the *Roe vs. Wade* decision, my pastor preached a message about abortion. At the end, he called forward everyone who has been affected by abortion. There were forty or fifty of us who went forward. He prayed for us and assured us we were forgiven. He kept saying the sin of abortion is 'covered by the blood of Jesus.' As a Christian, I know that's true, but I still feel bad. Even the kids have noticed something is wrong with me. One day, my six-year-old asked me why I'm sad all the time. That was probably my lowest point. Soon after that, I picked up a brochure about this program at a health fair. I couldn't believe there was a group like this. I thought it was too good to be true until I met Sofia and June."

Natalie studied Tanika's large hazel eyes that were framed by a broad forehead and high cheekbones. She thought Tanika could pass for twenty-two if only she would smile more than frown. *I can't imagine the trauma of being raped, then having an abortion,* Natalie thought, *but at least she has kids.*

"Thank you, Lisa," Sophia said. "We're glad you found out about the group. Donna, would you like to go next?"

Donna had been talkative earlier, but now it seemed she couldn't speak. She rubbed her hand through her brown, curly hair and began to cry.

"I'm sorry," she said. "I don't really want to be here, but I know I need to be here. Rebellion has always been a big piece of my life, and I have been fighting with myself all day about coming tonight."

Natalie was glad to know Donna also questioned whether she should be there.

Sofia reached over and touched Donna's arm. "Donna, coming here tonight is one of the bravest things you and the other women here could ever do. Starting out on this journey to talk about our abortion decisions and what it has done in our lives isn't fun. We all have ways to spend an evening that would be far more pleasant."

Donna smiled.

"Trust us that on the last night of this group, you will look back and be happy that you persevered. We're just so glad you chose to come tonight. Do you feel like continuing, or do you want us to come back to you?"

"It's okay. I'll go on," Donna whispered. "I was a PK, a preacher's kid, and for a while my mission in life was to do the exact opposite of what my parents said. Maybe it was because I was the middle child out of five. Who knows? I just remember being fed up hearing the same syrupy messages over and over again. God and Jesus and heaven seemed unreal to me. Ever since I can remember, my brothers and sisters followed the straight path that was laid out for them by Mom and Dad. I did, too, for the most part, but by the time I got to college, I was ready to party. In the midst of all that, I managed to find a decent guy who loved me and wanted the baby."

Donna shook her head.

"I couldn't handle it and screwed up once again by having the abortion. I always felt bad about the guy, but I wouldn't allow myself to think about the abortion. I never told anyone in my family. By the time I graduated from nursing school, I had a full-blown alcohol and drug problem. My parents were shocked. They're the ones who sent me to rehab the first time. Things began to look up. I moved to another city and got a job as, of all things, a labor and delivery nurse. I had buried my emotions so deeply, not even that bothered me, or so I thought. Finally, drinking got the better of me, and my employer forced me into rehab. Actually, they were quite supportive. I could no longer see patients, but as long as I stayed in Alcoholics Anonymous and passed periodic urine tests, I could work in an administrative job. This pattern continued. I would be sober and work successfully for a while but end up in a rehab again. During the best times, I was a good nurse. We're talking several different jobs and more than one suspension of my nursing license."

Donna looked away from the group and stared into space. June and Sofia sat patiently while Donna reflected and gathered her thoughts. Natalie didn't think she was alone in wanting to run over and give Donna a hug.

"Anyway, what finally broke me was a coworker's wedding. It was odd. As I sat in the sanctuary, I started to cry. People cry at weddings all the time, but not like this. I was sitting in the back, so it's not like I caused a big scene or anything, but I was definitely sobbing. I guess it was the combination of being in a church for the first time in a while and all the family stuff associated with that. Then, seeing this young couple in love, starting out life together—it was too much. I left before they said, 'I do,' and told my friend later that I had gotten sick.

"I cried nonstop for almost two days. It was a full-blown

breakdown. I got in to see my counselor as soon as I could. When I explained what had happened, he was useless. Nothing clicked. On the way home from that session, I swear God was sitting next to me in the car. He brought to my attention every major problem I have ever had. My entire life replayed in my head. At that moment, he showed me that the sadness in my life, my inability to form new relationships, especially with men, all stemmed from my abortion. I was checking things out on the internet and found information about postabortion stress, like we talked about earlier. When I mentioned this whole thing to my new counselor, she found out about this workshop for me. She's not a Christian, but she encouraged me to try it out. I give her credit for that. I figured I didn't have anything to lose, so here I am."

"That sounds like a series of miracles, Donna!" June said. "You may feel rebellious, but God is stronger than your rebellion, and it is obvious that he is the one who brought you here tonight. We're glad he did."

Natalie was humbled by everything Donna had been through. She thanked God she hadn't struggled with substance abuse. She began to see that God also had a hand in getting her to this group.

They all turned to the one who hadn't shared yet.

Chunky jewelry dwarfed Meredith's tiny earlobes and slender wrist. Blonde, highlighted hair hung perfectly straight and ended just above her shoulders. The ice-blue sweater she wore matched her eyes. Meredith's porcelain face was void of lines, frown, or smile. Natalie wondered if she was still a teenager.

Meredith took a deep breath and sighed. "I got

pregnant on a one-night stand. I'm not proud of it, but that's what happened. My abortion was three months ago. I would still be pregnant now. I used RU-486. The people at the clinic said it would be private, and it was. Private, bloody, traumatizing. I thought I would be relieved, but the image of the tiny, perfectly formed baby that came out of my body haunts me. I've started a new job that requires long hours, but all I can think about is how I've messed up my life. Both my brother and sister have toddlers, and I can't bear to look at those kids. I feel like I'm in a bad dream and can't wake up. I realize I can't go back, but I wish I could. That's all."

Natalie saw tears in the eyes of every woman around the table, except Meredith's.

June broke the silence. "Thank you, Meredith. We know it's very difficult to talk about these things so soon afterward. We're just glad you're here. And for the rest of you, we know it's hard for you, too, especially if this is only the first or second time you have told anyone. We realize it has been a long evening. There are just a couple more things before we call it a night.

"As happy as we are that you're all here," June continued, "the enemy isn't. He doesn't want you to be here, and he doesn't want you to come back. He wants you to continue to languish in shame, guilt, and hopelessness. This week, there are a couple of verses we would like for you to meditate on. First Peter 5:8 says, 'Be self-controlled and alert. Your enemy the devil prowls around like a roaring lion looking for someone to devour.' If your experience is like that of many others, the devil was there in the front row when you chose abortion, saying, 'Go for it, it's no big deal. Everybody has had an abortion. It's the only solution.' Then, after it was over, he said, 'What you have done is so horrible you can never tell anyone, and God will never forgive you.' That's the enemy devouring your hope.

"Now that you have decided to deal with this issue, you will doubt you can ever be forgiven or healed. You will second-guess yourself about coming to this workshop. This week, instead of giving the devil a foothold, meditate on 1 John 4:4, 'the one who is in you is greater than the one who is in the world,' and James 4:7, 'Submit yourselves, then to God. Resist the devil, and he will flee from you.' Be in prayer, and we'll be in prayer for you. God wants you to be free from the pain and sadness you've been experiencing."

"We're so glad you're here," Sofia said. "Do you have any questions before we close in prayer?"

The room was silent.

"June," Sofia said, "will you pray?"

"Dear heavenly Father, we thank you for tonight. We thank you for these women who have followed your prodding to seek help in resolving the feelings they have about their abortions. We thank you for the testimonies that were shared here tonight and for the love and respect you are developing among these women for one another. In the week ahead, give each of these women what they need. Direct them to your Word and keep their thoughts on you. Amen."

Sofia and Julia asked permission to hug each woman as she left the room. No one declined.

Natalie's head was swimming as she headed out the

door. She thought about the wonderful women she had met and how their stories touched her heart. She knew she caused a scene by crying so much, but, for the first time, she was able to tell someone about her abortion. As much as she dreaded sharing her experience, speaking the words out loud somehow lessened the power this awful secret had held over her for the past seven years. It was still a secret, however, from Randy. As she neared her house, she thought about what a drag it would be to pretend she was playing pickleball for the next seven Thursday evenings. Then it became crystal clear: she would have to find a way to tell her husband the truth.

As the week progressed, Natalie thought about the group in her private moments but never uttered a word about it to anyone else. She prayed for each of the women by name and in her mind rehashed their stories and their pain. She marveled at how God had repaired June's marriage and thought about the damage she was doing to her own. She was still embarrassed about breaking down the way she did and wondered what the other women thought of her, but she knew what June had said was true—she was among friends in that group. By the time the next Thursday rolled around, Natalie decided to hold off talking to Randy about her abortion.

CHAPTER 3

Truth

The Lord is close to the
brokenhearted and saves those
who are crushed in spirit.
—Psalm 34:18

Group—Week 2

"Gotta go," Natalie said. "I'll do the dishes when I
get home."

Randy called after her, "Have a good game."

Natalie drove to group with great anticipation,
anxious to see the women again and anxious to move
ahead with tonight's session. She felt badly about the
pickleball lie, but she wasn't ready to tell Randy. Not yet.

"Good evening, ladies," June said. "It's good to see
you. How was your week?"

Everyone nodded and smiled.

"Wait a minute. Who's missing?"

"We're missing Meredith," Sofia said.

"Maybe she's just running late. Did anyone here think about not coming back tonight?"

"Yes, ma'am, I did," Tanika said nervously. "Bringing up all this stuff is really hard. I want to get right to the part where I start feeling better."

Natalie knew what Tanika meant.

"An honest woman," June said. "Of course, this is hard. I think we warned you about that. We are in a society that values instant gratification. Isn't that how most of us got into this mess? We want this to be over yesterday and for all the bad feelings to go away. But it's a process. It makes me think of when you get a splinter in your foot and you don't get all of it out. The skin will heal over, and you think it's okay, but there's still soreness there. You keep walking on it. Then, the whole area around the splinter gets infected and the soreness gets worse and worse. Something has to be done. You realize it won't fully heal until you cut through the layers of skin and remove the source of the pain. In this group, you are opening that hurt, cutting through the layers of pain to get to the source of your misery—your abortions. It's not a pretty metaphor, but you get the idea."

"Well, I'm relieved to be here, to be finally dealing with this," Lisa said. "After last week's group, it felt like a huge weight was lifting from my shoulders. I realized before I got here this will be a process, but all I could do this past week was praise the Lord. I read my Bible and talked to a close friend a couple of times about what's going on. I'm excited about what the Lord is going to do in our lives through all this."

"That's terrific, Lisa," Sofia said.

Natalie felt a twinge of guilt. *I'm going to talk to Randy this week. I am,* she told herself.

"In spite of what I said earlier, I had a good week," Tanika said. "I'm glad I started this workshop. Of course, I knew that just physically getting to this group would be a challenge, and it has been. Last week when I got home, my kids, Deborah and Joel, had been fighting. Today, my babysitter called and said she couldn't come tonight. It worked out okay because the neighbor is watching them, but it has been challenging all along the way. Oh, then when I got in the car tonight, it wouldn't start. My brother brought me."

"The enemy doesn't want you here, Tanika," June said. "We're glad you made it."

"Thank you."

"What about you, Donna?"

"I can honestly say this group has already opened up so much about my behavior that I feel I'm on the brink of something very healthy, yet scary at the same time."

"Don't be scared, Donna! God is in charge of this group, and he's not scary. He will lead you gently where you need to go," June said.

Natalie made eye contact with June.

"Natalie," June asked, "do you have something to add?"

"Just that I'm still nervous about being here. I haven't told my husband yet, but I'm thinking about it. Because he doesn't know about the abortion—it was before I met him—it's more than just admitting I'm attending a workshop. Plus, I think it is probably because of the abortion that we can't conceive."

There. She had said it out loud. Her deepest fear was that her abortion had been the cause of her infertility.

"Did a doctor tell you that?"

"Well, no, not in so many words, but …"

"Don't do that to yourself, Natalie," June said. "There's at least two things going on here. You're blaming yourself for something that you don't even know is true, and you're selling your husband short by assuming he won't accept what you have to tell him. As we go through this group, Natalie, I believe the Lord will show you how to handle these issues. It will be okay. You've spent years not dealing with your abortion, years not telling your husband, and years of harboring these fears about your fertility. Now that you are dealing with them, it can seem overwhelming. Take it one day at a time."

Natalie felt tears once again. Sofia scooted a Kleenex box in her direction.

"Thank you," Natalie said.

"Let's pray," June said. "Lord, thank you for bringing us back to group this week. We thank you for your love for us and for being a God of forgiveness and redemption. Be with us tonight as we peel back more layers of the guilt, shame, and denial. We pray for Natalie and her concern over the issues she mentioned. Comfort her, Father, and give her the wisdom and discernment she needs to move forward. Prepare her husband's heart for helping her to come to grips with her past. We remember Meredith tonight and right now ask for your protection over her.

She needs you, Father, and she needs this group. Please break down the barriers, real or imagined, that have kept her from coming back tonight. We turn this evening over to you. Thank you for being here with us. Amen."

Natalie couldn't believe she had once again opened her mouth and shared her private desperation. She and Randy were scheduled to meet with the fertility specialist in a few weeks. She assumed up until now the infertility was her fault. She was sure that because of her abortion, something was wrong with her and that she would never be able to get pregnant. *Isn't that what I deserve? Could it be true that it isn't my fault?* Her heart leapt at the possibility.

Natalie's attention shifted to Sophia when she moved to the front of the room. "Tonight," she said, "we're going to talk about defense mechanisms. Those are the things that have enabled us to cope with our abortions for however long it has taken God to lead us to deal with them. It's a way of behaving that keeps what's really bothering us from surfacing. Who can describe for me a type of defense mechanism?"

"Well, do you mean something like denial?" Lisa asked.

"Exactly. You have heard the term that someone is in a 'state of denial' when they aren't acknowledging a certain occurrence or set of circumstances. The same can be true regarding abortion. We don't want to believe that we have done what we have done, so sometimes people will simply deny they have ever experienced abortion or have had any connection with anyone who has. Avoidance, another defense mechanism, goes hand in hand with denial. In order to deny our past, we avoid anything that will trigger memories. We may cross the street when we see a pregnant woman, or avoid a woman holding a baby. Someone last week mentioned that she can't look her own nieces and nephews in the eye. Oh yes, it was Meredith. Some people may avoid medical personnel and physical exams. Along with that, I have a question for you. How many of you have told the truth on the form in the doctor's office when you're asked how many pregnancies you have had?"

Tanika spoke up. "Now that you mention it, I've never told the truth. I have two children but have had three pregnancies. I never told my doctor about the abortion."

"You're not alone, Tanika," June said. "It wasn't until I was thirty-five years old and pregnant with my second living child that I decided I could face telling the truth."

Natalie squirmed. She hadn't told her husband *or* her doctor.

Sofia continued, "Another defense mechanism that many of us use is rationalization. You justify your behavior by saying things to yourself like, 'Having an abortion is the best thing I could do because …,' and you fill in the blank. The rationalization may be something like 'I have to finish school,' 'I just started a new job,' 'I can't afford a baby,' or 'My parents or my boyfriend will be upset.' Sound familiar?

"While rationalizing your actions, you may minimize the situation and say something like, 'It was just a blob of tissue,' or 'It's a simple procedure and no big deal.' Often your friends who know about your abortion will minimize it because they don't really want to talk about what happened either. They may tell you to get over it and go on with your life. As you look back on your own experience, I am sure you can see this is a primary tactic used by those who promote abortion.

"We may repress our experience and choose to not think about it. We may get so good at this that we have no memory of the incident at all unless it is triggered by a sound, smell, or vision. Some women can't run the sweeper because the sound reminds them of the suction machine. One of you—I believe it was you, Natalie—said the medicinal smell has always reminded you of your abortion."

Natalie nodded. Just the mention of it took her back to that day.

"I was the queen of repression," Sophia said. "I decided that if I didn't acknowledge my abortions, they would go away. It's a little game you play with yourself, but over time, it gets harder and harder to keep things pushed down inside of you."

Natalie realized in a flash that this was what she, too, had been doing in order to cope with her abortion.

"Another behavior among postabortive women is to have an 'atonement' baby to make up for the missing child. There is a deep desire to have another baby to replace, or make up for, the one who is gone. What often happens, though, is that the woman's circumstances remain the same, and when faced with another pregnancy, she may choose abortion a second time, further compounding the original problem.

"I'm sure that in some way, this desire led to my becoming pregnant a second time. As I shared with you last week, I had a second abortion. This can become a sad, futile pattern because, as we know, you can't replace a child. The child or children you aborted were created to be unique individuals.

"Another way we attempt to make ourselves feel better about our abortions is called 'bargaining.' This takes on one of two possible faces. A woman may become very pro-life to recognize, and to make up for, her actions. She may even try to prevent others from making the same mistake. The flip side of this is the woman who becomes stridently proabortion to attempt to justify her decision by supporting or helping others make the same decision.

"I am willing to bet," Sofia said, "that a majority of the women working in abortion clinics are postabortive. It's a way to make yourself feel better and a misguided way to help other women.

"Some of us play the blame game and place all the responsibility for our abortion onto someone else. This isn't to say that others haven't had a role in our decisions, but the responsibility is ultimately ours. The person using this mechanism says, 'I'm not responsible. So-and-so made me do it. It was So-and-so's decision, not mine."

"Most of us have a lot of anger surrounding our abortions. This, too, is a way to mask our true feelings of sadness and betrayal. Someone pointed out to me once that my sarcasm was a form of anger. Now, that made me *really* angry! Seriously, though, that comment caused me to listen to myself and realize how negative and sarcastic I had become. It was a way, I believe, of keeping people at bay. We will talk lots more about anger over the course of the workshop."

"Thank you, Sofia," June said. "That's a good

overview. You know, using these mechanisms hasn't made you a bad person. It means you're human. You used them to protect yourself, to survive the trauma of abortion and its aftermath. After a while, however, it takes a lot of emotional energy to keep the lid on our feelings.

"How do we break out of the negative patterns we've developed since our abortions?"

"Confession?" Lisa asked.

"Yes! That's the best starting point," June answered. "It says in 1 John 1:9 that if we confess our sins, God is faithful and just and will forgive us our sins and purify us from all unrighteousness. *If* we confess, he will do these things for us. Confession involves acknowledging the fact of our abortion or abortions and acknowledging that abortion is sin. First, we must confess. Then, we must believe. Do you believe that God can forgive you and cleanse you?"

Natalie squirmed in her chair. It always seemed as if Sofia and June were speaking directly to her and no one else in the room. She hoped it was a rhetorical question.

"The defense mechanisms we've been using helped us protect ourselves from the reality that we destroyed our babies. God wants to replace those mechanisms with the truth of his forgiveness. In John 8:32, the scripture says, 'Then you will know the truth and the truth will set you free.' Four verses later it says, 'So if the Son sets you free, you will be free indeed.'"

I know the truth, Natalie thought, *but Randy doesn't. How I wish I had told him a long time ago. I've got to make this right. I can't continue to go on like this.*

"Let's take a break," June said. "I was in charge of

the refreshments tonight, so there's chocolate and more chocolate. Make it quick though. We still have a lot of ground to cover tonight."

There hadn't been much time in this session for interaction with the other women like last week, so Natalie was glad to be able to chat with the others and have a snack at the same time. They talked about the material they had just heard. All of them commented on the lies they had told over the years to hide their abortions.

"It would be funny—all the stupid things I've done— if it weren't so sad," Tanika said.

Natalie thought about her phantom pickleball game.

"Well, if nothing else, this group has already shown me there's a lot of us in the same boat," Donna said. "Let's just be glad we're here now and dealing with things."

"Amen to that," Tanika said.

"Let's go, ladies," June called into the kitchen. The women took their seats, and June resumed the session by asking a question.

"Have any of you considered that the fears in your life are a result of your abortion? I never thought about this until I went through this group. Fears go hand in hand with defense mechanisms. For instance, if you're trying to suppress the memory of the abortion, there may be a fear of disclosure. So, the fear of facing our abortions is the very thing that causes us to hang on to the defense mechanisms that we've just talked about. The use of denial, avoidance, and rationalization becomes a vicious cycle.

"Other common fears are fear of intimacy, fear of medical personnel, fear of infertility, fear of the opposite sex, fear of the future, and fear of God's punishment.

Natalie, just tonight you shared with us your fear about infertility. I know from my own experience that, following my abortion, I was fearful of relationships with men."

Natalie recognized her life was ruled by fear. Fear of their upcoming doctor's appointment and fear that she was the cause of their infertility. Fear of telling her husband about the abortion and fear of what would happen when the truth was revealed. She began to jot down her fears in her notebook.

The women discussed the fears each of them had experienced and how they had coped with them. They went around the room and took turns reading aloud several scriptures that serve as antidotes to fear:

Joshua 1:9

The Lord is my light and my salvation—whom shall I fear? The Lord is the stronghold of my life—of whom shall I be afraid? (Psalm 27:1)

He will cover you with his feathers, and under His wings you will find refuge; his faithfulness will be your shield and rampart. You will not fear the terror of night, nor the arrow that flies by day. (Psalm 91:4–5)

Peace I leave with you; my peace I give you. I do not give to you as the world gives. Do not let your hearts be troubled and do not be afraid. (John 14:27)

> For God did not give us a spirit of timidity,
> but a spirit of power, of love and of self-
> discipline. (2 Timothy 1:7)

Natalie's favorite was the one about finding refuge under his wings. *That's where I want to live*, she thought. The part about the shield and the rampart was disconcerting, but she knew enough about the Bible to know that God considered life a battle. She leafed through her Bible until she found what she was looking for, Ephesians 6:11–17:

> Put on the full armor of God so that you can take your stand against the devil's schemes. For our struggle is not against flesh and blood, but against the rulers, against the authorities, against the powers of the dark world and against the spiritual forces of evil in the heavenly realm. Therefore put on the full armor of God so that when the day of evil comes, you may be able to stand your ground, and after you have done everything, to stand. Stand firm, then, with the belt of truth buckled around your waist, with the breastplate of righteousness in place, and with your feet fitted with the readiness that comes from the gospel of peace. In addition to all this, take up the shield of faith, with which you can extinguish all the flaming arrows of the evil one. Take the helmet of salvation and the sword of the Spirit, which is the word of God.

I am in a battle, Natalie thought, *a battle for my emotional health and for my marriage.*

"We're going to move right into talking about your homework, because we have several things for you to do this week," June said. "First, reread the information we've given you about defense mechanisms. Don't think about them in an abstract way. Think about which defenses and which fears apply specifically to you. Identify which ones have colored your life since your abortions. As you investigate these feelings, we want you to go a step further. You are going to do a lifeline. These can be enlightening, but they take time. I'm going to try to explain what to do. Then I'll show you mine to give you an idea of what we're looking for.

"You can call this exercise a lifeline or memory map of significant events in your life. You're going to take a piece of paper, turn it sideways, and draw a straight horizontal line across the middle of the page. Place a dot at the far left side of the line, which represents as far back as you can consciously remember. I think I identified a memory of when I was three years old, which really surprised me. Place another dot at the far right end, which represents the present. In between, in chronological order as best as you can, place a dot for each significant event, label what it stands for, and also date it. Place your positive event dots above the line at the height that will reflect how happy and positive that event was. Likewise, place your negative event dots below the line at the depth that reflects how hurtful or negative each event was. Then, from left to right, draw a line that connects the dots. You'll end up with something that looks like this," June said, as she held up her own lifeline.

It resembled a map of hills and valleys. Natalie thought about how anxious she had been to get to group tonight, but now it was no longer interesting or helpful. Things were getting uncomfortable. She didn't like reliving the past. It was hard enough dealing with today. She remembered the commitment she had made to go through this group, but now she wasn't so sure. Then she remembered what Sophia said about crying all the way through the first group she attended. *No one said this would be easy. I guess if Sophia and June both got through this, I can too.*

"I'm really old, don't forget," June said, smiling, "so when I did this, I discovered one of the most significant events in my life was when our neighbor's son was killed in Viet Nam. I was only nine years old, but he was someone I knew and saw daily. Our families were close. To this day, I remember my mother and Mrs. O'Malley sitting in our living room crying. I didn't understand why it happened, which made it very confusing and scary. Our family was not particularly emotional, so I was taken aback by the outpouring of grief. That incident and all the news about the war led to a lot of fear in my life," June said as she pointed to a dot on her lifeline.

"Interestingly, that happened a few years before I went through preparation classes at church and was confirmed. I placed so much significance on that process, yet it didn't seem important to my parents. They sent me so many mixed messages about church and their expectations of me. It was soon after that I began to have problems with them and began to turn to boyfriends for my primary relationships. I became sexually active right after high school, and in college had my abortion. I was also able to look back at all the opportunities my mother had to speak to me about sex but didn't. That lack of communication and lack of preparing me resulted in a lot of my anger toward her."

Sofia spoke up. "I can tell you this exercise was one of the most meaningful things I did in group. My only word of advice is to be totally honest with yourself. That is the way you will derive the most benefit. This exercise can reveal areas of hurt and confusion that you may have carried into your relationships with your babies' fathers. The negative traits and behaviors modeled for you in your families may have been magnified in your relationships. Doing these lifelines can also help you renew positive feelings about experiences in your life that have helped shape you."

"Do you have any questions?" June asked.

"You want us to write down every good and bad thing that has happened in our whole lives?" Tanika asked with a quizzical look on her face.

"Well, not every good and bad thing," June said, "just the most significant ones. And it's up to you to decide which events are significant. For example, you shared with us about the rape. I'm presuming that occurrence and your subsequent abortion were a couple of the most negative occurrences in your life. On the positive side, there were the births of your children. Other significant events may have to do with education, job, relationships, or your spiritual life. Make sense?"

Tanika nodded her head.

"Don't forget," Sofia said. "You can call either one of us during the week if you have questions. You have our numbers. Also, I don't think we had a chance to talk about this last week, but we encourage you to journal throughout your experience with this group. It will help get your feelings out, and it will help you with your homework. If you haven't journaled before, start with just a paragraph or two a day, whatever you're comfortable with. Putting this lifeline together may inspire you to start recording your feelings. Does anyone here already journal on a regular basis?"

Journaling. Natalie journaled once for a class. *How could I ever keep a journal without Randy finding out?*

"I do," Donna said. "It has been part of my therapy for a long time. I just make a point to record some of the occurrences of my day, and it naturally leads to more. If some days I don't write a lot, it's not a big deal, but I usually write something every day. It helps me crystallize things in my mind—how things fit into the big picture of my life. Plus, I include prayers and reflections on things that God is doing. It's neat to look back and see the good things that are happening and how I've dealt with the bad things—sometimes well, sometimes not so well."

"I used to," Tanika said. "With two young kids, I've gotten out of the habit, but I used to enjoy it. I'll definitely try it again."

"Great," June said. "Well, ladies, give journaling a try this week, and don't forget to do your lifeline. Sofia, will you close us in prayer?"

"Lord, thank you for bringing us back together tonight. We pray for Meredith and ask that you guide her back to this group. Please be with her as she comes to grips with this issue. Please provide Natalie, Tanika, Lisa, and Donna with encouragement and strength as they delve into difficult issues. Bring to their minds the significant events in their lives that may unlock something important. Be with them, and thank you, Lord, for your grace and mercy. In Jesus's name. Amen.

"One more thing," Sophia called out. "Remember that last week I said I'm a crier? I have a handout for you that is called, simply, 'Tears.' That's it. See you next week, and don't forget that you can call either of us if you have questions about your lifeline."

Again, Sophia and June stood by the door so they could hug each participant as she left the room. This week, the participants hugged one another too.

"Bye, Tanika," Natalie said. "Have a good week."

"You too, girl. Hey, are you still playing pickleball?" Tanika smiled.

Natalie smiled back because she knew Tanika was teasing her and didn't realize she'd hit a nerve. "Well," Natalie hesitated, "my pickleball days are going to come to an end soon. See you next week."

"Thank you for everything you've shared, Natalie," Donna said to her as they walked to the parking lot.

"Oh, Donna, thank you. You've been so brave to share everything that's happened to you."

"It's not bravery. It's surrender. I finally realized I don't have the answers, and they're not at the bottom of a wine glass. Letting go of things and turning them over to God is the hardest thing I've ever tried to do, but already it has given me a new lease on life."

"That's great," Natalie said. "I'm trying too. It's a little scary."

"Remember what we talked about tonight, the verse from Timothy ... God has given us a spirit of power, of love, and of self-discipline."

"You're right. That's one I'm committing to memory. Thanks, Donna. Have a great week."

When Natalie got to her car, she read the handout Sophia had given them.

Tears

Tears in scripture play a unique role in spiritual breakthrough. Here we discover that the planting of seeds accompanied by a spirit of brokenness will not only bring a spiritual harvest of results but will leave the sower with a spirit of rejoicing in the process. This passage, along with numerous others in scripture regarding a spirit of brokenness, pictures a variety of purposes and functions related to what might be termed "the ministry of tears," a ministry Charles H. Spurgeon (a famous nineteenth-century British pastor) defined as "liquid prayer." First, there are tears of sorrow or suffering (2 Kings 20:5). Second, there are tears of joy (Genesis 33:4). Third, there are tears of compassion (John 11:35). Fourth, there are tears of desperation (Esther 4:1, 3).

Fifth, there are tears of travail, or giving birth (Isaiah 42:15). Sixth, there are tears of repentance (Joel 2:23, 13). Passion in spiritual warfare is clearly needed (Numbers 10:1–10, Ephesians 6:10–18).

Natalie grabbed the pocket-sized Bible she kept in her purse and quickly looked up the scripture references. Just reading about tears made her cry. She still felt embarrassed by crying so much during the previous week's session, and this made her feel better. She wiped her tears, then started the car for her drive home from her "pickleball game."

Natalie stared at the beginning and ending dots on the piece of paper. It seemed strange to boil down her life to dots on a page. She was an only child and had been happy ... until she got older. She couldn't remember anything remarkable. What *was* her first memory? She thought about their dog, Max, and remembered trying to climb on his back. She must have been about three or four years old. That was her first memory. She made a dot and wrote down *Max* at the far left of the page. She remembered having fun with her mother and winning a look-alike contest at the mother-daughter banquet at church when she was eight years old. Then there was the time her dad lost his temper with her and with her Little League coach. She hadn't thought of that in years.

Her dad was a perfectionist and had little patience for her mediocre attempt at softball. He must have thought the coach was mediocre too. Natalie liked her coach. He made sure all the girls got to play. Natalie remembered that on the day in question, she made the last out in the last inning, and her team lost. She remembered feeling bad about it, but not as bad as she did when her dad ran over to her and yelled at her to get in the car. She hadn't understood why he was so mad. "Do as you're told," he had screamed at her. His yelling brought her to tears. As she turned to walk to the car, she heard her dad rip the coach. He used language she had never heard him use before. He told the coach he shouldn't have let her embarrass herself like that. Didn't he know how to teach batting? Wasn't he there to win? What did they do at practice anyway?

She noted the events on her timeline. She reflected on her dad's perfectionism and how it affected her performance in school. She seldom received less than an A in anything, but if she got a B, he would question why she had been so lazy and hadn't been paying attention. She didn't want to find out what it felt like to get a C.

Her mind drifted to when she began her love affair with basketball. She remembered the first organized game she played in when she was in sixth grade. She marked it on her lifeline. She felt like she was flying when she played ball. A year later, when she made the middle school team, she begged her mother not to tell her dad. She remembered his behavior from her days in Little League. Around the same time, her father said that if she didn't stop growing, she'd never find a man tall enough to marry. Mom had told her he was just joking, but she didn't think so. To her, he was saying she was some kind of unfeminine, amazon freak. The comment stung because basketball made her feel, for the first time in her life, comfortable in her own skin. Her height was an asset, and she definitely wasn't butch. Why couldn't her dad be happy for her that she found something she enjoyed and was good at? Basketball became her identity, something her dad always seemed to want to crush. Nothing he could say would deter her, although he tried again to interfere with her coach once she got to high school. Coach Evans set him straight immediately, and she respected and admired him for it. In a way, he insulated her from her father. Plus, her dad had nothing to complain about. She kept her grades up, and she excelled at basketball. She received every award there was for individual performance, and the last two years of high school, her team advanced to the state finals. That had a lot to do with her getting a scholarship.

Her family had never been especially religious, but the summer before she left for school, she went to a girls' basketball camp where a professional player spoke about accepting Christ. Natalie had accepted Christ when she was a little girl, but this athlete had something she didn't: a personal relationship with Jesus. Then, a couple of months later, she met Ned and didn't have time for other relationships. *Oh God,* she thought, *I really made a mess of things. Please forgive me.*

As Natalie went back and wrote these things on her lifeline, she could see a pattern of perfectionism and people-pleasing that began early in her life. She saw that, just as she was growing into her own identity apart from her parents, and as soon as she got away from home, she fell for someone just like her dad. Ned was fanatical about his appearance and hers. He was a scholar and was fiercely competitive when it came to grades and opportunities. A baby out of wedlock didn't fit Ned's perfect image of what life, at least his life, should be. As for her, she realized the fear of her dad's condemnation, along with Ned's, prevented her from doing what she knew was right. She looked at the completed lifeline. It took her from the innocence of the family dog to baring her soul in a workshop for postabortive women. Overall, she thought it looked rather dismal but, for once, her faith was stronger than the brokenness of her life. She knew God had brought her to this place for a reason. She had to trust him for the healing she so desperately needed in her life, and she had to trust him for her marriage. She knew she may have married Randy for all the wrong reasons, but he was a good Christian man who loved her just the way she was. She felt a renewed sense of love and appreciation for him.

Natalie was again eager for the next week's group.

Anger

> But now you must rid yourselves
> of all such things as these: anger,
> rage, malice, slander, and filthy
> language from your lips.
> —Colossians 3:8

Group—Week Three

"Welcome, everyone," June said. "Let's open in prayer. Heavenly Father, thank you for these women. We know this group provides many challenges, but we know that you will be with each of these ladies every step of the way. Thank you for our discussion last week about defense mechanisms and fears. Be with us tonight as we review our lifelines and move on to the next topic. Also, please be

65

with Meredith. We miss her and wish her well. In Jesus's name, amen."

"How did you do with your lifelines?" Sophia asked.

"It was interesting," Lisa said. "I was surprised with what I came up with. This is hard to talk about, but I need to. For a long time, I blocked out the verbal and emotional abuse I experienced as a teenager. I was never sexually abused, but my household was sexually charged, for lack of a better term. Once I began to develop, my dad couldn't keep his hands or eyes off of me. You know how they say it's healthy for parents to hug their kids? Well, in his case, it wasn't healthy or fatherly. It was lecherous. As I worked on my lifeline, I remembered practically the day I realized my daddy wasn't my daddy anymore."

Lisa brushed away a tear.

Natalie listened intently to what Lisa was saying. *At least my father didn't do that,* she thought. *He was just a control freak.*

"I was in constant fear he was going to rape me. I loved my mother, but she was a weak person and powerless to control him. She may have been afraid of him too. Anyway, I spent a lot of time at girlfriends' houses, and I left home the day after I graduated to elope with my high school sweetheart. I went from the home of my bully father to the home of my bully husband. Then we had our babies almost immediately. Some of the best times in my life were when the girls were little."

At this point, Lisa held up her lifeline and pointed to the area when she was a young mother.

Lisa continued, "I didn't begin to grow up emotionally until my first husband and I were divorced and I was on my own. I felt so fortunate to meet Chuck. Like I said once before, I didn't want to rock the boat by angering him when he said he wanted the abortion. Even though I usually stand up for myself, I seem to be compliant with men—usually out of fear of harm or rejection. This exercise helped me see that, and it also reminded me how strong and self-assured I felt when I was on my own. I'm not suggesting that I want a divorce, but I realize now that I need to appreciate that part of me and let it out in positive ways. Coming here to acknowledge my babies is one way. This exercise really opened my eyes to how the things that happened to me as a kid affected me in later life."

"Lisa," June said, "you have put a lot of work into this. Go back a minute to the situation with your mother. Did you ever resolve with her the fact she didn't protect you from your father?"

"We never really talked about it. No."

"Later, we're going to move into a discussion about anger, and when we do, we will want each of you to identify people with whom you're angry. In addition to your dad, Lisa, you can be thinking about any anger you have been harboring toward your mother."

"Who would like to go next?"

"I will," Tanika said. "I found myself getting caught up on good things that happened to me prior to the rape and my pregnancy. As you mentioned last week, the rape was a turning point. Before that, I got all As in school. I received awards for perfect attendance, awards for science projects, and awards for spelling bees. My great-aunt attended every assembly and program and always had a party for me on the last day of school to celebrate my achievements. Those were good times. After my abortion, I hardly ever went to school. I flunked tenth grade, dropped out, and ended up getting my GED. Getting into community college was a high point, and meeting my future husband was a good thing, at the time."

"What about your great-aunt?" Sofia asked. "Did you ever have good times with her after your abortion?"

"Not really. She was always part of our lives. She helped me a lot with the kids, and she was always over for holidays, but she and I seldom talked or laughed together. It's too bad."

"Yes, Tanika, it is. She obviously loved you and your children. Hold up your lifeline for us."

Tanika briefly explained each peak on the sheet and the significant dip that led her to seek out the healing workshop. Natalie marveled at God's goodness in bringing each of them to that point of surrender that Donna had spoken about last week.

"Donna, what about you?" Sophia asked.

"Well, there were parts of this exercise I enjoyed, and other parts were not fun. And doing this sober was … sobering." Donna chuckled.

Donna started to unfold her lifeline. "Anyway, on the limited positive side, I was able to remember some warm moments with my mother when I was little. My dad too. That meant a lot, actually. Then I remembered a very specific incident with one of my sisters. We were playing and broke my mother's lamp. My sister lied about what happened, my mother believed her, and I got blamed. I know this was one of many such incidents, because I remember this being the last straw for me. It was at this time that I wrote off anyone in my family believing me, and I was still just a kid. The only positives I have after this are school related, not family related. And then here is where I started drinking, and here is my abortion," Donna said as she pointed to two specific low points on the lifeline.

June pointed at the paper. "It looks like there are several high points after that. What are they?"

"This one is a guy I met and had a relationship with. These two are jobs that I started and really liked—until I started drinking again. This is when I started going to AA the last time, and I'm still going, by the way. This one at the end of the page is now. It's this group."

"That's a thorough job," June said. "Was it worth doing to rediscover some of the positives in your life?"

"Oh, yeah," Donna said. "It was a gift to remember some of the early days with my family when things were happier. It was also a gift to realize how far I have come."

"Natalie, how did yours go?"

"It was fun and sad at the same time," Natalie said as she displayed her lifeline. "There were several good things I remembered that I hadn't thought of in years, but I quickly discovered there's a thread of perfectionism that runs through my family, including me. I have this desire to do well and to please everyone all the time. I never want to disappoint anyone, ever."

"That's a tall order for anyone. What happened when you weren't able to please people?"

"Well, of course, I felt guilty and worthless. I'm beginning to realize how this pattern of people-pleasing played right into my abortion. I wanted to please Ned rather than stand up for myself and our child. I can't believe how deceived I was, not that I want it to sound like I'm blaming him." Natalie choked back a sob. "All I'm saying is I better understand now about why I behaved the way I did, and it's what brought me to this point in my life. It's time for a new beginning and time for me to learn a different way to interact with people. Like I mentioned to Tanika last week, I've got to lose the pickleball game and come clean with my husband about where I go every Thursday night."

"You will, Natalie. Ladies, let's pray for Natalie right now."

Sophia walked to where Natalie was sitting, stood beside her, and put her hand on Natalie's shoulder. Natalie closed her eyes and bowed her head. Sophia hesitated a moment, then began.

"Lord, it says in your Word that you have given us a spirit of power, not a spirit of fear. Right now, we ask you to break the fear and people-pleasing that has ruled this woman's life for such a long time. You also tell us that we shall know the truth, and the truth will set us free. This marriage needs the truth. Give her the strength and the words she needs to talk to her husband. Go before Natalie and prepare her husband's heart. Protect and strengthen this marriage. And right now, Lord, we ask you to bless this marriage with children. Give Randy and Natalie the desire of their hearts. Let this marriage and this family be a testament to your grace and mercy. In your son's name we pray. Amen."

Tears streamed down Natalie's face. She immediately

tried to remember everything Sofia had said. She knew the verse she prayed from 2 Timothy—"For God did not give us a spirit of timidity, but a spirit of power, of love and of self-discipline"—was beginning to take on a special significance for her.

"Okay, ladies. Let's take a break." Natalie sat there for a moment and dried her tears. Her heart was full with emotion from sharing the lifeline and from Sofia's prayer on her behalf. She was excited about what was happening in this group. She knew she was being stretched emotionally and spiritually. They all were. She had heard people say, in relation to a church or Bible study experience, that "God showed up." She had never really understood that before, but she did now. That was what was so special about these Thursday nights. God showed up!

Lisa came over and hugged her. "C'mon. Let's get something to nibble on."

After the break, Sofia began a discussion about anger. "Anger is a feeling we have all felt before. Some of us verbalize our anger, and then it's over. Some of us hold on to anger for months or even years. It becomes a black cloud over our lives. We take out our anger on the wrong people, and we can become bitter, miserable people. The abortion experience can lead to this type of unresolved, intense, lingering anger. What about you? Do you have feelings of anger?"

There were nods around the room. Sofia continued, "With whom are you angry? Why? When did this begin? How is this affecting your life today?"

June stood by the flip chart and said, "We're going to

make a list of the people with whom you're angry about your abortion. Who wants to go first?"

"I do," Tanika said. "I'm angry with my great-aunt for forcing me to have the abortion."

"Okay," June said as she wrote "great-aunt" on the paper.

"My mother," Donna called out. "And my father," she added. "While I was growing up, all I heard were religious platitudes. It seemed as if they didn't live what they believed. They were caught up in pride and appearances, just like anyone else. I was an embarrassment to them. Every time I went home on break from school, I managed to do something that 'mortified' them, and that's their word. I knew I couldn't go home pregnant out of wedlock. Everybody wants to think their parents love them unconditionally, but I never did."

"What about your siblings?" June asked. "Other than the sister who blamed you for breaking the lamp, I don't think I've heard you say much about your relationship with them."

"We didn't have much of a relationship, although I don't look back on them with as much anger as I do my parents. If anything, I felt sorry for my siblings because they were missing out on effective parents as much as I was."

"I'm maddest at myself," Lisa said. "I knew what I was doing was wrong, but I let myself go with the flow instead of standing up for myself and my babies. It goes back to what I said about being compliant and seeing that modeled for me by my mother. That's not an excuse, but I can see now how that played into my frame of mind."

"In this group, we are dealing specifically with our abortions, but so many things you have mentioned point back to your mother. Just now you said that she modeled compliant behavior for you. Are you sure you're not just a little angry with her for that?" June asked.

"Well, yes. I am."

"What about the people at the clinic? Do any of you need to forgive the doctor who performed your abortion or the nurses who assisted?

The women nodded. Donna said, "I'll never forget the receptionist at the clinic. I was the only one in the lobby, and she was trying to reassure me. While I was filling out the paperwork, she talked to me about when she 'needed' to have her abortion. I have never forgotten her choice of words. Now, when I look back on that, I feel sorry for her, and it makes me mad at the same time."

A long-forgotten memory bubbled up in Natalie's mind. "I don't even remember the doctor's face," she said, "but when it was over, he told me I could 'go out and party again in six weeks.' What did he mean by that? Was it supposed to be a joke? Here I was, totally traumatized, and he was equating sex with partying. I couldn't tell you his name, but I've hated him for that remark ever since. I need to forgive him. He really didn't know what he was doing or saying." Natalie quit talking and looked down. It took a moment for her breathing to return to normal.

June wrote down "doctor."

"You know, the people who work in these clinics need our prayers. Think about how deceived they are. They make their livings by selling death, and they think they are helping people. The clinics are dark places. Have you ever noticed how the windows in these clinics are either covered or nonexistent? There's a great verse in Ephesians about this. Let me find it," June said as she picked up her Bible. "Here it is. Actually, there are several verses about darkness, but I'll read Ephesians 5:11–14. 'Have nothing to do with the fruitless deeds of darkness, but rather expose them. For it is shameful even to mention what the disobedient do in secret. But everything exposed by the light becomes visible, for it is light that makes everything visible.' That's why we're here. We're shining light on all the dark places."

"No one has mentioned the obvious one," Sofia said.

"The baby's father," Lisa said. "I know that, down deep, I'm still mad at Chuck. Oh, we've worked through a lot of things in our marriage, and he's a good man. But when I reflect on how he thought we were too old, I ask myself what we have done in the time since the abortions that has been more important than raising kids. The answer is nothing."

"I would also say my baby's father," Natalie said. "His rejection of us started me on a downward spiral, and I'm just beginning to understand the repercussions. Him and my dad."

"I tried to move on emotionally, especially after I got married," Tanika said, "but yes, I was and still am angry with Dwayne. Just look at my lifeline. There was a giant dip after the rape. The last I heard of him, he ended up in prison, so I always felt that he was worse off than I was, but it was cruel the way he stole my innocence."

"Is anyone angry with God?" Sofia asked.

"Not anymore," Tanika said, "and I can't really say I

was ever mad at him. There were times when I wondered where he was, but I was maddest at my great-aunt."

"Donna, you're a PK. Did you blame God?"

"At the time, I'm sure I did. Most of my outward anger was directed at my parents, but in a way, I was jealous of God. I felt my parents weren't tuned into me because of their dedication to him. Luckily, since the time of my abortions, I have matured as a Christian. I have been able to separate a lot of my feelings about how my parents were as parents from what it means to be a healthy Christian, but I admit I cried out to God in anger and despair more than a few times."

June wrote down "God." "This is a good list," she said. "If you think of anyone else, we can add them."

"What do we know about anger?" Sofia asked.

"It's negative," Donna said. "It can consume your life."

"Yes, it can," Sofia said. "Let's see what the Bible has to say on the subject."

Sofia gave them each a verse to look up and read out loud. After a couple of minutes, Sofia said, "Lisa, go ahead."

"'For as churning the milk produces butter, and as twisting the nose produces blood, so stirring up anger produces strife' (Proverbs 30:33)."

Tanika read the following: "'Do not be quickly provoked in your spirit, for anger resides in the lap of fools' (Ecclesiastes 7:9)."

This verse hits too close to home, Natalie thought as she read, "'Get rid of all bitterness, rage, and anger, brawling and slander, along with every form of malice. Be kind and compassionate to one another, forgiving each other, just as in Christ God forgave you' (Ephesians 4:31–32)."

Donna read, "'Do not take revenge, my friends, but leave room for God's wrath, for it is written: It is mine to avenge; I will repay, says the Lord' (Romans 12:19)."

June finished by reading, "'For man's anger does not bring about the righteous life that God desires' (James 1:20)."

"All right, ladies, it's time to end for this evening. This has been a good week. I pray that, if he hasn't already, the Lord will bless you for all your hard work on your lifelines. This week, we want you to continue to journal, and next week we will resume our discussion about anger."

Sophia closed in prayer. "Lord, thank you for tonight. Thank you for everything you are revealing to these ladies, and thank you for drawing them closer to you. Be with them this week as they consider what your Word says about anger. Protect them, protect their marriages, and their children. In Jesus's name. Amen."

After hugs all around, Natalie headed for the door. She noticed Donna praying with Tanika in the corner. She thought about Donna, who had been through so much, giving so much of herself to the group. She thanked God for this group and for the ladies she had met. She saw Jesus in each of them. Natalie's peaceful meditation was interrupted as she neared her house.

"Oh, God," she said aloud. "I know I'm not supposed to be afraid, but I'm so exhausted, I'll make a mess of things. Next week. I'll talk to Randy next week. I promise."

CHAPTER 5

Forgiveness

> Be kind and compassionate to one
> another, forgiving each other, just
> as in Christ God forgave you.
> —Ephesians 4:32

Group—Week Four

*A*nother week went by. As Natalie was getting ready to leave for group, she thought about telling her husband what was going on. *Just blurt it out*, she thought, but then she realized she was running late and knew the conversation would take time. She donned her workout clothes and hurried out the door. *I have to stop this*, she told herself.

Prayer was already underway when Natalie walked into the meeting room.

Sofia ended with, "And thank you, Lord, for Natalie getting here this evening, even if she's late. Amen."

Everyone chuckled as Natalie took her seat. She was glad she hadn't gotten into it with Randy.

"How was your week?" June asked.

"It was great!" Lisa said. "Doing that lifeline really opened some things up for me. Unpleasant things but things I needed to deal with. It helped me understand why I was so vulnerable to making the abortion decisions. I'm not blaming my dad, or my mother, or my husband, because I was a grown woman when I made those choices, but it is amazing how family circumstances can negatively affect your thinking."

"What about your anger?" Sofia asked.

"I was angry with my dad for a long time, and my husband. Thankfully, I've had time to come to grips with that, but I can't say it's totally gone."

"That sounds like an honest answer, Lisa," June said. "Did anyone else think about anger this week?"

"I'm still angry with my great-aunt and with that fool who raped me," Tanika said. "That's what bugs me the most. I can't seem to get past the anger. I told you the guy is in prison, but that was for something else. Bottom line, in my heart, I still want my pound of flesh, but the good Lord tells me he'll take care of it. The other thing I always wonder about is what would have happened if I had told Auntie Jo right away and we had filed charges against him. He was still a juvenile. Maybe if he had been sent away, he could have gotten help. So, here I am, seventeen years later, blaming myself for the guy hurting others because he wasn't rehabilitated. It's hard to let it all go."

"Yes, it is," June agreed, "but that's something we're going to work on tonight and in the weeks ahead. Letting go of it and turning it over to the Lord is the one thing that will allow you to move forward and not fall back into relying on your old coping mechanisms. Thank you for sharing, Tanika. Anyone else?"

"I agree with Lisa about the lifeline," Natalie said. "It showed me a lot about who I am and the influences in my life. It got me back in touch with the side of me that used to be confident and sure of herself. I still have a lot of anger directed toward the father of my baby, but I have a lot of anger directed at myself, too, for being so stupid."

"You all know the lifeline was an eye-opener for me," Donna said. "I want a few more peaks in my future and not so many valleys. I can't say I'm still angry with anyone; at least, I don't think so."

"It's a valuable exercise," June said, "and you all worked hard on it. I'm glad it opened up some positive memories and some new perspectives. You may want to go back and look at it from time to time or add to it. It was important to do this because tonight we're going to talk about forgiveness. What is it? Forgiveness is freeing another person from the payment for an offense they have committed against you. Withholding that forgiveness is what leaves us in bondage—bondage to coping mechanisms, bondage to sin, and bondage to emotions."

"The thing we need to realize about forgiveness," Sofia said, "is that it is truly more for your benefit than for the other person."

"That's easy to say but not to do," Natalie surprised

herself by saying. "I was devastated by what Ned did to me. I still am."

Natalie realized she must feel comfortable with these women or she never would have offered this insight into her feelings.

"I understand, Natalie, but by forgiving Ned, it doesn't let him off the hook with God, nor does it result in reconciliation; you're doing it to clear up your own standing with God. Think vertically," Sofia said as she made an upward motion with her arms. "By forgiving others, you're first fixing your vertical relationship with the Lord. Healing the horizontal relationships with the people who have hurt you may or may not happen."

Natalie had never heard forgiveness explained this way and wasn't sure she understood.

Sofia continued, "Forgiveness is a decision, an act of the will. You can't base forgiveness on your emotions or on what the other person is doing. It's a choice, plain and simple. Once you make that choice, your emotions will eventually follow, and the Lord will bless your decision. I know this is hard because we don't think about forgiveness in these terms. We tend to hold forgiveness over someone's head and grant it if, and only if, we feel they have redeemed themselves and finally deserve it. Do you want God to do that to you? Natalie, Ned will never be worthy of your forgiveness, just like you and I can never be worthy of God's forgiveness. Let's flip to Matthew 6:14–15. Lisa, will you read it?"

"Sure. It says, 'For if you forgive men when they sin against you, your heavenly Father will also forgive you.

But if you do not forgive men their sins, your Father will not forgive your sins.'"

"That's incentive enough for me to work on forgiveness," Sofia said. "I mentioned reconciliation a moment ago. Forgiveness is *not* the same as reconciliation. Let's look at Tanika's situation, for example. We want Tanika to be able to forgive her rapist, not be reconciled to him. That's another way we get confused about forgiveness. Forgiveness is not granting access to us or permission to hurt us again. To be freed, you must forgive and release those you are angry with."

"Hmm," Natalie said. "I have spent a lot of time thinking about how much I hate Ned for what he did to me, but I haven't found much time to think about forgiving him."

"That's an important revelation, Natalie," June said. "It takes energy to hang on to that hatred. More than any other reason, we need to forgive others and ourselves for our own sakes. Unforgiveness can lead to resentment and bitterness. Have you ever met someone who is filled with bitterness? It's an ugly, unhappy thing. God wants more than that for you. Forgiving is hard work, and it's a process. It's an act of your will. Like Sofia said, the emotional changes will follow. If I waited until I *felt* like forgiving my baby's father, I'd be stuck in a twenty-five-year-old time warp. It is the act of forgiveness that allows the Holy Spirit to do the work in us."

"I have lived this," Lisa said. "I had so much resentment built up against my husband I could barely stand to look at him. At one point, I thought the only thing left to do was to divorce him. Then, one day, I realized we are the same.

He and I are both sinners who have fallen short of God's best. Even though I blamed him, I realized God loves *him* as much as He loves *me*. And, if God forgives *me*, then I need to forgive my *husband*. If I claim to have Jesus in my heart, who am I to be holding grudges against people? It was hard at first, because I wanted Chuck to hurt like I did and have the same feelings I had, but that was never going to happen. Letting go of that expectation was the best thing for me and for our marriage."

"That's awesome, Lisa," Sofia said. "What about God's forgiveness of us, like Lisa mentioned? Tanika, please look up 1 John 1:9."

Tanika flipped to the far right of her Bible. "Okay, here it is: 'If we confess our sins, he is faithful and just to forgive us our sins and purify us from all unrighteousness.' That's a good verse."

"Yes, it is, Tanika. Natalie, please look up the last couple of lines of Jeremiah 31:34."

"'For I will forgive their wickedness and will remember their sin no more.'"

"Thank you. Did you hear that? God not only forgives; he does what is humanly impossible—he forgets. Donna, please read Psalm 103:8–13."

"'The Lord is compassionate and gracious, slow to anger, abounding in love. He will not always accuse, nor will he harbor his anger forever; he does not treat us as our sins deserve, or replay us according to our iniquities. For as the heavens are above the earth, so great is his love for those who fear him; so far as the east is from the west, so far has he removed our transgressions from us. As a father has compassion on his children, so the Lord has compassion on those who fear him.'"

Natalie took a deep breath. "How can we *know* if God has forgiven us?"

June answered her in a quiet voice. "Honey, we know it through the Bible, through those verses we just read. And there are many others. Have you ever asked God to forgive you?"

The question made Natalie feel uncomfortable, and she was sorry she brought it up.

"Of course I've asked God to forgive me," Natalie said defensively. Then her voice lowered, and she asked, "But how can I be sure?"

"Do you believe he's forgiven me for my abortion?"

"Yes."

"Do you believe he has forgiven Sofia and Tanika and Donna and Lisa?"

"Yes."

"Then, let me understand," June said, "are you saying the God of the universe, the Great I Am, the omniscient, omnipresent Father sent his only son to die for everyone's sins but yours?"

Natalie was stunned. She felt foolish and knew her ears were red. She was hurt that June had been so blunt with her in front of the other women, but the truth pierced her heart. Tears welled up in her eyes.

"I see your point," Natalie whispered.

"I think each of us has had the same thought at one time or another. It's a form of pride the enemy puts in our minds. We talked about it in our first or second session. We become convinced that what we did was so awful and so terrible that not even God can forgive us. Romans 5:8 says, 'But God demonstrates his own love for us in this: While we were still sinners, Christ died for us.' Jesus died on that cross for you, too, Natalie. He took on the sins of everyone in this room that day on the cross, and it is finished."

"Amen. Thank you, Jesus," Tanika said.

Donna said she also had felt at one time she could never be forgiven. Tanika, Lisa, and Sofia piped in, and each said she had felt the same way. Natalie didn't hear their words. She was still taking in everything June had said. *Pride.* The enemy had convinced her she was so much worse than any other sinner that she couldn't be forgiven, no matter how many groups she attended or what her pastor preached. *Pride.* The enemy had convinced her that she was so much worse than any other sinner that she discounted the cross and the nature of God. She had been duped—duped into believing that having an abortion was no big deal, then duped into believing that her very soul was lost forever.

Natalie looked down at her hands. Physically, she looked the same, but something inside was different. June's words had brought her back to reality. She felt strengthened. She was going to walk in the truth and no longer believe the lies of the enemy.

"There is a great scripture that describes the desperation of not feeling forgiven by God," Sofia said. "Lisa, please read Psalm 32:1–5."

"Okay. 'Blessed is he whose transgressions are forgiven, whose sins are covered. Blessed is the man whose sin the Lord does not count against him and in whose spirit is no deceit. When I kept silent, my bones wasted away through my groaning all day long. For day and night your hand was heavy upon me; my strength was sapped as in the heat of summer. Then I acknowledged my sin to you and did not cover up my iniquity. I said, "I will confess my transgressions to the Lord"—and you forgave the guilt of my sin.'"

"What was that?" Natalie asked. "Could you read that again?"

Lisa read it again, and Natalie gasped. "Oh, my gosh. The part about 'my bones wasting away through my groaning all day long.' I've read that before, but I'm looking at it with new eyes."

"That nails it," Tanika added.

"Let's take a break, ladies," June said. "I need a cup of coffee!"

Natalie remained seated, deep in thought, until Donna touched her shoulder. "Are you okay, Natalie? It's time for break."

"Donna, can you believe it? I actually thought God couldn't and wouldn't forgive me. I thought I was going to hell."

"Isn't God good? He knew that in this group, for the first time in your life, you would hear and understand the truth about his forgiveness. He loves you, and he knew what you needed."

When the ladies returned from break, June was ready to explain their homework.

"This week, your homework is to write letters expressing your forgiveness to the people you need to forgive. These aren't to mail! This is an opportunity for you to say all the things you want to say to people who may be gone, or to people you don't really know, like the doctors or nurses, or to people you're not ready to talk with in person. If you want to mail them at a future time, that's fine, but during this group, these letters are just for you. You can write as many as you want, but you are expected to write at least one. We'll ask you to share one or more of them next week. Sofia and I will each share one of ours to give you an idea of what we're talking about."

June began to read the letter she had written to her husband:

> Dear Joe,
>
> You have been a good provider and a good father to Alison and Jay. From the outside, I'm sure most people would say we have the perfect life, the perfect marriage. What they don't know is the secret we share—the secret of my abortion before we met.
>
> The worst part is, because you have never been willing to talk with me about it after I told you, I have felt resentment toward you. Maybe you resented me first because I brought this baggage into our marriage. I don't know. But in case you haven't noticed, it has been difficult for me to bond with our kids because I felt I didn't deserve to have them, let alone have a relationship with them. I have been

angry because so many times I felt you and the kids shut me out, and I was jealous of your relationship with them. I'm the one who has kept people at bay and survived on surface relationships. I forgive you for not wanting to talk to me about my abortion. Why would you? I approached everything with such anger and such a chip on my shoulder. Please forgive me for blaming you for my unhappiness about my abortion. I look forward to the day when we can talk about this openly with one another.

Love, June

"This letter really helped. I think I told all of you before that once I went through this group and I brought up the subject with him again, he had no idea it was such a stumbling block for me. He prayed with me at that time, and now he is supportive of my doing these groups."

"Did you ever give him the letter?" Tanika asked.

"No, but just through the exercise of writing it, I realized how much the abortion had affected our marriage. That gave me the courage to approach him in person."

Sophia cleared her throat and began.

Dear Mom,

I am writing to tell you that I forgive you for the part you played in the two abortions I had. When I was pregnant the first time, you suspected it and said, "If you're pregnant, you're getting an abortion." I never let you know, but I *did* have the abortion. Your comment was the first blow of rejection I felt in those crazy, mixed-up weeks and months. I will never know what would have happened if you had said, "If you're pregnant, we will love both you and the baby and will help you through this." After I became a Christian, your actions seemed even more hurtful, and I harbored a growing resentment toward you. When I thought about the fact you never once talked to me about men and dating when I was young and needed your guidance the most, I became even angrier at you.

Once, in counseling, someone suggested to me that people from your generation were taught that it was unacceptable to talk openly about sex. That helped me understand and forgive you.

I'm sorry about my abortions for many reasons, but one reason is that I denied you ...

Sofia's voice trailed off. Natalie looked up to see tears streaming down her face. Tears immediately came to her own eyes. She grabbed a tissue for herself and pushed the box in Sofia's direction. Sofia put a tissue to her face and sobbed. Now Natalie noticed tears in the eyes of every woman around the table. No one spoke. After a while, Sofia began again.

> I'm sorry about my abortions for many reasons, but one reason is because I denied you two more beautiful grandchildren. They would have benefited from knowing you, and you them. It helps to know they will know you in heaven. God has helped me forgive you, Mom. I know you loved me and took care of me the best way you knew how.
>
> Love, Sofia

Sofia sighed. "You know," she said quietly, "it never goes away. Abortion never goes away. Sin is like a rock thrown into a pond. The sin may be gone, but the ripples from that sin are far-reaching and long-lasting. We have God's grace and mercy to thank for bringing us to this point. We know one day there will be a reunion with our children, but here and now, our lives are forever changed. The only way to heal our relationships with the people involved, and with God, is to begin the process of forgiveness."

June asked if anyone had questions about the homework. Hearing none, she closed in prayer: "Heavenly Father, it's hard. It's *still* hard. We know abortion never goes away because the consequences of our sin—the deaths of our precious children—are real. These and other consequences, like what we've done to ourselves and others in the aftermath, are redeemable only through you. Your forgiveness of us and our forgiveness of others can make all the difference. As you taught us to pray, forgive us our sins as we forgive those who sin against us. Forgiveness is your will for us. We must choose forgiveness, even when our feelings don't match up. Be with us this week, especially as we meditate on the issue of forgiveness and write our letters. We ask you for safe travel and to bring each of us back next week. In the name of your precious son, Jesus. Amen."

The women lingered and talked for a while before leaving.

CHAPTER 6

Unconditional Love

But while he was still a long way
off, his father saw him and was
filled with compassion for him;
he ran to his son, threw his arms
around him and kissed him.
—Luke 15:20

Group—Week Five

"Let's pray," June said. "Heavenly Father, we ask for your Holy Spirit to be with us here tonight. As our subject matter becomes more difficult and personal, we ask for perseverance for these ladies and their desire to see this group through to completion. Thank you for being with us. In Jesus's name. Amen.

"Natalie, you look like you're about ready to burst with excitement. What's going on?"

Natalie knew her smile was giving her away. "I have something to share."

"Great. Let's hear it."

Natalie wanted everyone to understand the full impact of what had happened, but she wasn't sure where to begin. *Just say it!* she told herself.

"During our first meeting, I mentioned that I was telling my husband, Randy, I was playing pickleball on Thursday nights. Last week when I got home from group, I couldn't stand it anymore. I was lying to him, just another consequence of not dealing with this whole issue. I finally told him everything, All about the abortion and all about this group."

"Natalie, that must have taken a lot of courage," Sofia said. "What was his reaction?"

"I was scared to death, as you can imagine, and I just kept talking and talking and barely looking at him. He finally just grabbed me and held me, and we cried together. He was shocked, but his overall reaction was better than I could have ever hoped for. When I told him I was afraid that what I had done was keeping us from getting pregnant, he said we would deal with it together when we meet with the doctor. He said he was sorry for everything I had been through and sorry I felt I couldn't tell him. I know he needs more time to process everything, but he was understanding and nonjudgmental. If the situation had been reversed, I don't think I could have been as gracious. I'm not naïve. I know this isn't an easy thing for a marriage, but I'm relieved to finally be honest with him. Neither of us shut down, and I'm happy about that."

"Go, Natalie! That's great," Donna said.

Lisa reached over and squeezed her arm. Tanika smiled and asked if this meant she didn't have to continue to pretend she was playing pickleball on Thursdays.

"No more Thursday-night pickleball games," Natalie answered. "Now I can quit wearing sweats to these groups!"

"Congratulations," June said. "Telling your husband was a huge step."

"How about everyone else?" Sofia asked. "How was your week?"

"Nothing like Natalie's!" Donna said.

"What about your homework? Who would like to read her letters?"

Tanika caught Sofia's eye. "I have a letter," she said. "It's to my great-aunt."

"Go ahead, Tanika," Sofia said.

Dear Auntie Jo,

You had no idea the damage you were doing when you forced me to have an abortion. For a long time, I thought you just didn't want to be embarrassed, but I know now you thought you were protecting me. When I was a little older, I found out from Aunt Lou that you had her when you were barely fourteen. You had to quit school, and you didn't want that for me. You also had a lot on your hands raising Antonio and me. (Antonio is my brother.) I don't know how you did as well as you did, especially with money being so tight.

It has been hard for me because it hurt so much to have someone I loved and trusted make me abort my baby. First, I was raped and got pregnant, and you wouldn't understand or talk about it. Then, it felt like rape all over again when I had the abortion. And we never talked about that either.

I have had trouble with my anger toward you. I've felt that way even though I know you would have done anything in the world for me and the kids. You need to know that I forgive you. My feelings don't always match those words, but I *do* forgive you, and my feelings will catch up over time. You've been gone for eighteen months, and it still seems strange not to be able to talk to you in person. But, one day, we will talk in heaven, and our understanding of each other and our love for each other will be perfect. I love you, forgive you, and miss you.

Tannie

"That was beautiful, Tanika," Sofia said. "Tannie. Is that what your great-aunt called you?"

"Yes."

"Was this a difficult letter for you to write?"

"It was. I always felt intimidated by my aunt, and I never wanted to cross her. As a result, I have never liked confrontation. To me, this was as if I was confronting Auntie Jo, even though she isn't here. I was always fearful of hurting her feelings or bringing up subjects that she wouldn't like. So, even though it was freeing to be able to say these things, it felt like confrontation."

"You expressed yourself very clearly and respectfully, Tanika," June said. "You acknowledged you forgive her, even though your feelings may not be there yet. It was a good letter."

"Thank you. You know, I also had something of a revelation as I wrote this. As I mentioned my great-aunt and I didn't talk much about anything, but as I was writing, it occurred to me that she must have been raped too. I knew she was only fourteen when she had my aunt, but that was before I was born, and I never knew if she had been married or divorced. If that's what happened, I know she thought she was sparing me lots of heartache."

"You may be right. If nothing else, I hear empathy in your voice for your aunt, something I haven't heard before," Sofia said.

"I guess that's the revelation part," Tanika said.

"Would you like to go next, Lisa?" June asked.

"Sure. This letter is to my husband."

Dear Chuck,

Our precious babies would be teenagers now. I am so sorry I aborted them. I am sorry I have blamed you for my decision to end their lives. I forgive you for your reaction to our first pregnancy and telling me I should abort. I know that if I had stood up for them and for myself, they would be here today. But, at the time, you had your reasons, and I didn't disagree. I used those reasons as rationalization for my own decisions. I know you feel badly about this. I can tell it's hard for you to talk about it, but you have been supportive of my decision to come to this group. I love you, Chuck, and am so happy that we both know the Lord now. It is only through Jesus Christ that you and I can each find forgiveness and peace. I want that for our marriage. I love you and forgive you. Please forgive me.

Love, Lisa

"I don't want the death of our babies to also kill our marriage. It's important to me that Chuck understands how I feel because I think it's important to be able to tell our story to others. Just by sharing my testimony at a women's retreat, God used it. Not because it was me or my story but just because I had the guts to bring up the subject. Several women at that retreat came up to me at different times afterward and admitted to having had abortions. That encouraged me to share my story with others, but my marriage is the most important thing right now. And I want to tell you something else."

"What?" June asked.

"I know these letters are supposed to be just for us, but I gave mine to Chuck."

"You did? What did he say?"

"I sat down with him and told him there was something I wanted him to read. At first, I thought he was going to get mad, but he didn't. He said it had been so long ago that he was surprised I brought it up. He had no idea it was still bothering me. He told me he didn't mean to hurt me and didn't realize it was such a big deal. I tried to explain from a mother's point of view, and from God's point of view, what it meant and how it had affected me. Anyway, Chuck told me he was sorry. Hearing those words from him was what I wanted more than anything in the world. He said he loved me and supported me talking about it at church if that's what I want to do. I really pressed him on that point because I don't want my outspokenness to be hurtful to him."

"Lisa, that's great. Do you think you and Chuck will be able to talk about this more openly now?"

"We'll see. I'm just thankful for his reaction to me. Like I said, more than anything, I needed to hear him say he was sorry, and he did. I'll be there for Chuck if he wants to talk about it more but, like most men, he's not much of a talker. As for me, I need to talk things out. I think that's what's so great about being able to share your story and your feelings in a group like this. I think we help each other more than we realize just by sharing and by listening."

"I agree with you, Lisa," June said. "That's exactly what makes groups like this work. Thank you for sharing your discussion with Chuck. Wow. There have been some really good things happening this week! Donna, will you go next?"

"Yes. I wrote two letters. One letter is to my parents, and one is to Gary, the father of my baby. I needed to tell my parents I forgive them, and I needed to ask Gary to forgive me. Is that okay?"

"Sure, Donna. Go ahead."

"I'll read Gary's first."

> Dear Gary,
>
> Please forgive me for aborting your baby. I had no right to make that decision without you. I know you wanted the baby, but I didn't listen.
>
> In addition to the baby, I know I also destroyed the dreams you had for us. Please forgive me for my selfishness. You were a wonderful friend and a loving man. I could see only what I wanted at the time, and even that was distorted by my drinking and drug use.
>
> I think of you often and hope you found happiness with a wife and family …

Donna began to cry.

"Take your time, Donna," June said gently.

"I'll be okay," Donna said through muffled sobs.

Natalie felt a wave of sympathy for Donna. She thought about where Donna had been in her life and how far she had come. After about a minute, Donna resumed.

I would want that for you and would feel terrible if I thought what I did kept you in any way from moving on with your life. If it is any consolation, I truly believe Romans 8:28—that in all things God works for the good of those who love him, and who have been called according to his purpose. At this point in my life, I can say without reservation that I am called according to his purpose, and I trust you are as well. I am healing now from my self-destruction, including the abortion and disregard for others. I praise God for that and ask for your prayers and forgiveness.

Fondly,
Donna

Donna sighed.

"That was very nice Donna," June said. "Whenever you're ready, go ahead with the letter to your parents."

Donna blew her nose, then continued.

Dear Mom and Dad,

I have blamed you for many, many things in my life. Maybe you didn't realize that the way you talked to me and about me turned me into the black sheep of the family. You must have known I was the butt of jokes and ridicule from you and my brothers and sisters. If I protested,

99

it was because I didn't have a sense of humor or I was being too serious. The things you said to me hurt me deeply. It made me a stronger person, and for that, I guess, I should thank you. But in addition to making me strong, it made me bitter. What really tore me up was your religious hypocrisy. There was Dad, a pastor and confidant to many, and you, Mom, a leader of women's Bible studies and a Sunday school teacher. Neither of you had time to talk to me. You didn't know me, not the first thing about me. I was lonely in my own home.

Now, I no longer blame you. I am writing to tell you that I forgive you for all of it. Sure, sometimes I catch myself playing the same old tapes in my head and looking to place blame elsewhere for what has happened to me, but I know I can't do that. It's false thinking. If Jesus can forgive me for my sins, I can and must extend forgiveness to you both.

I love you.
Donna

"It sounds like you covered a lot of ground in that letter, Donna," Sofia said.

"It was definitely cathartic," Donna said as she smiled a half smile.

"May I ask," Sofia said, "are you close to any of your siblings?"

"Geographically, I haven't been close to either of my sisters or my brothers since I left for college. I don't think they missed me, and I certainly didn't miss them. In my mind, I lumped them together into one worthless unit that I sometimes see and tolerate on holidays. Then, about six months ago, my younger sister called and asked if she could come visit me. I was shocked. To make a long story short, she also has problems with substance abuse. We talked and shared, for the first time, about our childhood and what went wrong. We're still not what I would call close, but I enjoyed that time with her."

"I'm glad. Being able to share with your sister after all this time must have seemed like a gift."

Donna nodded. "It did."

"Natalie, are you ready to read your letter?" June asked.

"Okay," Natalie said. "This letter is to Ned, and I want to warn you about it. I knew I was mad at him, but once I started writing, I discovered how much. I still have a long way to go with this forgiveness stuff."

"That's okay, Natalie," June said. "We all have to start somewhere."

Dear Ned,

It has been a long time, but almost daily I think of you and of our child. I still can't believe what a jerk you were. I know you were scared, and I know you were pressured by your parents to do well in school and become a doctor, but that was no excuse. You were cruel. You took total advantage of me and our situation. I would love to know if you ever became a doctor and if what happened to us affected the rest of your life, like as it has mine. I guess it doesn't really matter, though. What matters now is my healing.

In order to do that, I have been told I need to forgive you so that I can be set free. It doesn't seem fair that's how things work, but I know it's true. So, while these words may not sound sincere, they are. I acknowledge my part in our unhealthy relationship and the abortion. It was a difficult time for both of us, but I hope by now you know we made the wrong decision. So, from this day forward, I choose to release the hatred I have felt for you, and I make the choice to forgive you.

Natalie

"You've taken some huge steps this week," June said. "How do you feel about what came out in that letter?"

"It was hard to write and hard to physically type the part about forgiveness. Afterward, it felt good. I kept thinking about what you said last week and what several of us have mentioned tonight: the shift in emotions follows the act. So, my forgiveness is an act of will. The feelings aren't quite there yet," Natalie said.

"And that's okay," June said. "They will come. Let's move ahead with our new material for tonight. Sophia?"

"We're going to talk about our image of God and how that image may be tainted by the feelings we have about our earthly fathers. And in doing our lifelines a couple of weeks ago, it was apparent that some of us, I guess all of us, have had dysfunction in our relationships with our dads. Let's talk about this for a minute. Stop me if I'm putting words in anyone's mouth. Natalie, you mentioned your dad was demanding and judgmental. Donna, you said your dad was aloof, and tonight in your letter, you said he was a hypocrite. Lisa, you left your home in fear of being abused by your dad. And, Tanika, your great-aunt raised you—your dad wasn't around."

Everyone nodded.

"So, what do these life experiences do to our view of a heavenly Father? Anyone?"

"I guess I never really thought about it much," Lisa said. "Once I became a Christian, I knew the Lord was my refuge. I didn't confuse him with my earthly dad."

"That's good. Anyone else?"

"My relationship with my dad may have been part of the reason I found it so hard to believe God could forgive me," Natalie said. "Like Lisa, I hadn't really thought about that before, but it makes sense."

Natalie remembered her dad's yelling about anything and everything. She thought about the times he said she would never amount to anything because of a minor misbehavior or less than an A in a subject. She was thankful for the distinction between him and her heavenly Father, which was becoming clearer as time passed.

"There have been ups and downs in my relationship with God the Father," Tanika said. "We were raised in church. Let me tell you, we were always in church. I guess I questioned a lot of things. I questioned why everyone was all lovey-dovey in church and then could turn around and be mean. I questioned why my mom and dad weren't around. I questioned how much God really loved me. I questioned why he let me get raped, and I questioned why he let my great-aunt treat me the way she did. Only, you weren't allowed to question anything out loud at our church—or in our home, for that matter. These were questions I asked myself and God. It wasn't until later when I got into a different church and I started to grow up as a Christian that I began to understand that God is a loving God, but the world is the world. We're all sinners, and we mess up. I've tried not to hold anything against God. He's cool."

Everyone laughed.

"Yes, he is," Sophia said. "Donna, what about you?"

"I think I said before, I was jealous of all the time my mom and dad spent with church stuff. I was jealous of God. As you can imagine, my problems with my parents, especially my dad, affected my relationship with God. I walked away from him. It's that simple."

"Thank you for sharing, everyone," June said. "I think there are times when each of us becomes overwhelmed with life and ambivalent about God. Fortunately, God is never ambivalent about us. We've all experienced disappointments with our earthly fathers when they have let us down. God never lets us down. Let's see what the Bible says about his relationship with us."

"In Hebrews 13:5, God said, 'Never will I leave you; never will I forsake you.' A couple of verses later, it says, 'Jesus Christ is the same yesterday and today, and forever.' Think of that. There's a constancy and consistency about Jesus that we can never find in another person, not even a parent.

"In Psalm 139, it talks about how reassuring his presence is. Verses 7–10 read, 'Where can I go from your Spirit? Where can I flee from your presence? If I go up to the heavens, you are there; if I make my bed in the depths, you are there. If I rise on the wings of the dawn, if I settle on the far side of the sea, even there your hand will guide me, your right hand will hold me fast.'

"Psalm 34:7 says, 'Delight yourself in the Lord and he will give you the desires of your heart.' What are these verses getting at?"

"He wants a relationship with us," Donna said.

"Exactly," June said. "The Creator of the universe desires to spend time with me and with you. How does he know the desires of our hearts? Because we tell him! Ladies, are you spending time with God? Are you developing a relationship with him? Are you climbing up on his lap where you're safe and pouring out your soul to him?" June paused to let the questions sink in.

Natalie thought about it. She realized that, just as she acted with her husband, she didn't open up enough with the Lord. She knew she was missing out on a lot in both relationships.

"Maybe you couldn't do that with your earthly father,

but God the Father is waiting for you," Sophia said. "In Proverbs, it says about God, 'Those who seek me find me.'"

"Amen. Thank you, Jesus." All heads turned toward Tanika as she said these words. Most of them followed with their own audible "Amen."

"Do all of you know the story of the prodigal son?" June asked.

"Know it? I've lived it," Donna said.

Each woman nodded her head.

June continued, "The father in that story is extraordinary and may not be much like our own fathers, but he is a picture of God's love for his children. At the sight of his lost son, the son who squandered his inheritance and was living with pigs, the father starts rejoicing and plans a party to celebrate his return. This is not what my own dad would have done. This is a picture of God's love. Our sin is forgiven, and we are welcomed home.

"I can't stress enough that you have to be clear about your relationship with the Lord. If you have problems in this area, now is the time to deal with them. God desires simply for us to be in relationship with him. His grace and his mercy—not giving us what we deserve—can seem too good to be true, but that is the nature of our God."

Donna began to weep. "It's too much, isn't it?" she asked amid sobs. "It's hard for us to comprehend God's goodness. It's hard to believe he loves me so much that he is willing to write off the horrible things I've done. He is so different from what we encounter in the world. It's incredible."

"Can we take a moment to pray?" Sofia asked.

"Yes, let's," June said. "Go ahead, Sofia."

"Lord, never let us forget that you sent your son to die on the cross for our sins, any and all of them. We are thankful this is not just something written in your Word but something we can actually feel and experience. Keep our hearts humble, Lord, and teach us. Teach us how to accept your gift of forgiveness so that we can forgive others. Your Word says we love because you first loved us. We can forgive ourselves and others because you first forgave us. Thank you for loving us and forgiving us. Amen."

"Speaking of forgiveness," June said, "Sofia and I are going to read several scriptures about God's forgiveness. Then we'll take a short break before we get into our homework assignment."

Natalie closed her eyes and listened as June and Sofia alternated reading the scriptures:

"'When we were overwhelmed by sins, you forgave our transgressions' (Psalm 65:3)."

"'Come now, let us reason together,' says the Lord. 'Though your sins are like scarlet, they shall be as white as snow; though they are red as crimson, they shall be like wool' (Isaiah 1:18)."

"'Blessed are they whose transgressions are forgiven, whose sins are covered. Blessed is the man whose sin the Lord will never count against him' (Romans 4:7–8)."

"'For I will forgive their wickedness and will remember their sins no more' (Hebrews 8:12)."

Natalie's eyes popped open at the sound of June announcing, "Only five minutes for the break, ladies; we're running a little long this evening." She gathered with the other women in the kitchen to grab a drink and a snack before returning to her seat.

"For your homework this week," June said, "we want you to write a letter to God asking him for forgiveness for your abortions. And if you have any anger toward God hidden away, now is the time to ask for forgiveness for that too. I think our tendency is to say, 'Of course, I don't blame God.' But think back to when you found out you were pregnant when you didn't want to be, and then think about the abortion experience. What were you thinking about God then? Also, in your letter, we want you to acknowledge that you understand God has already forgiven you. Again, we know this through his Word, as in the verses we just read."

Natalie knew immediately that she would use Isaiah 1:18 in her letter. It was both poetic and personal. She loved the concept of the Lord beckoning her to sit down with him to talk things over.

"Sofia and I will share our letters," June said.

"It was difficult for me to get started on this letter," Sofia said. "Not because I didn't realize that I needed to ask God's forgiveness but because I didn't know where to start. You'll see that I relied heavily on Bible verses."

Dear Lord,

I am thankful to have come to a deeper understanding of you in recent years and to the knowledge that you have forgiven me my "iniquity," as it says in Jeremiah 31:34. I am still ashamed of myself when I think of how I avoided you and refused to come to you about my abortions because I thought you couldn't or wouldn't forgive me. Imagine! The omniscient Creator who numbers the hairs on my head not being able to forgive me. I finally realized it was a matter of pride and denial that kept me from you. Also, fear. The enemy had me so scared. Scared that if you didn't forgive me—and I didn't think you could—that there would be no hope for me. Instead, I learned in Joel 2:13 you are slow to anger and in 1 John 2:12 that my sins are forgiven.

I also remember a time when I *did* blame you for the messes I was in. I couldn't figure out why you let things happen, and I used to think, *If only God would do ... whatever.* Forgive me for thinking that then, or if I ever think it again. I'm the one who made the decisions, not you. It was convenient to blame you. Your gift of free will is such a loving, deep, wonderful thing, and I abused it.

My children are very missed in this world, but I know they are with you. Thank you for sending your son Jesus to die for my sins.

Your daughter, Sofia

June began her letter:

Dear Heavenly Father,

I go to a church where the pastor said several times that we shouldn't ask you for justice, we should ask you for mercy. He says it when he's trying to make a point, and some people chuckle knowingly. It took me a long time to figure out what he meant. My dad always liked to say that people get what they deserve in this life. He had a strong work ethic and high expectations of everyone, especially his kids. If we brought home bad grades or got into trouble of any kind, he would get really mad. Screaming and yelling were usually followed by the silent treatment until our mother intervened and got him to lighten up.

So, even when I devoted my life to you, I didn't have a reference for understanding mercy. Unconditional love and forgiveness of sins were foreign concepts to me. Then, through Bible study and prayer, I began to learn how different you are from my dad. I was fascinated when I read 1 John 1:9, which says, 'If we confess our sins, he is faithful and just, and will forgive us our sins and purify us from all unrighteousness.' It seemed too good to be true. Then I read Psalm 103:12, 'As far as the east is from the west, so far has he removed our transgressions from us.' That sealed it for me.

I confess my sin of abortion, Father, and ask for your forgiveness and mercy. Unlike my earthly father, I know you won't give me what I deserve but the peace and forgiveness you desire me to have. Thank you.

June

"After I wrote this letter, the very first thing that popped in my mind was a verse from the Bible when Jesus was talking to his disciples. It's John 14:27, and it reads: 'Peace I leave with you; my peace I give you. I do not give as the world gives. Do not let your heart(s) be troubled and do not be afraid.' I felt like that was God's response to me."

Peace. That's what each of us needs, Natalie thought to herself. *Peace about our babies, peace about what God thinks of us, and peace about our relationships.* She could see how being honest with Randy was already beginning to bring her a sense of peace she hadn't felt before during her entire married life.

"Do you have any questions about your homework?" June asked. "Remember to read over the scriptures in your notebook about forgiveness. That will give you a starting point if you get stuck. Sophia, will you close us in prayer?"

"Lord, we are thankful that you are gracious and merciful. We thank you that you are the God of

111

restoration and redemption and that in you we have a chance to start over. We rejoice with Natalie at the bold step she took this week, and with Lisa in sharing her letter with her husband. Protect and strengthen the marriages represented here, strengthen us as parents, and keep us close to you. Bring us back safely next week. We pray these things in your son's name. Amen."

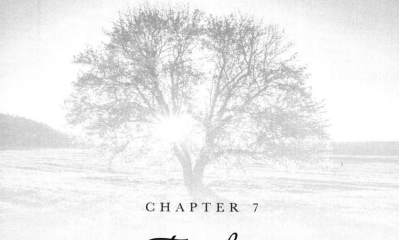

CHAPTER 7

Freedom

He has sent me to bind up the
brokenhearted, to proclaim freedom
for the captives and release from
darkness for the prisoners.
—Isaiah 61:1

Group—Week Six

"Welcome, everyone," June said. "Let's start with prayer. Heavenly Father, we thank you for who you are and for the healing you are bringing into our lives. Be with us tonight as we share with each other and as we grow in our knowledge of you. In Jesus's name. Amen.

"How was your week? Is anyone ready to share her letter to God?"

"I will," Natalie said.

Dear Lord,

In your Word, you say that if I confess my sins, you will forgive me and purify me from all unrighteousness. I never believed that before. I wasn't calling you a liar. I just thought what I had done was so awful, not even you could forgive me or would want to forgive me. I am so sorry that I doubted you. I gave the enemy more credit than you. Now I know what the verse means that says, "Greater is He that is in you than he that is in the world."

And I love you for saying that though my sins were like scarlet, you have made them white as wool.

I know now you have forgiven me for my abortion. Please forgive me for doubting you.

Thank you for directing me to this group.

Natalie

"That's very nice, Natalie," June said. "I liked the way you worked scripture into your letter. How was it to write this letter?"

"It felt good, hopeful. Learning more about God's forgiveness has changed everything."

"As it does for each of us. That's wonderful! Donna, would you like to go next?"

"No, but I will. I have to admit I didn't realize how

bitter I felt about my parents and God. I started to rewrite the letter to share with all of you, but then I decided to let it all hang out."

"I believe you mentioned bitterness in your letter to your parents last week, but you seem to be on your way to forgiveness. Did something happen in the past week?" June asked.

"No, except maybe I wasn't being totally honest about my feelings until now. I think my letter to God will make it clear."

"Okay. We'll listen."

Dear God,

I know I need to ask you for your forgiveness, but where's the forgiveness I deserve to receive from others? Where was my parents' forgiveness while I was growing up? Where was their understanding? Where was the communication? Where were they? How could they claim to love you so much but be so cold toward me? It seems as if by forgiving them, I'm just letting them off the hook. I have always wanted them to suffer the way I have, to feel how miserable I have felt, but they have been oblivious to all that. They have felt nothing but embarrassment because my life somehow diminishes theirs. Because of me, they are less perfect, less successful than they felt they deserved to be.

"Okay," Donna said, "here comes the good part."

> But, as I write this letter, it occurs to me
> that you have felt my pain, you have felt
> my misery, you have felt my isolation. It
> occurs to me that you have loved me even
> when I was unloving toward you. It also
> occurs to me that Romans 5:8 applies to
> me in a personal way: "But you, God,
> demonstrate your love for me in this:
> while I was still a sinner, your son Jesus
> Christ died for me." The other verse that
> rings true is that if I don't forgive others
> their sins, you will not forgive mine. So,
> Lord, please forgive my self-pity and my
> desire for vengeance. I am nothing and
> can do nothing without you. Then, all
> things are possible, including forgiving
> my mom and dad.
>
> I also ask you to forgive me for
> destroying your creation—my child—
> and my attempt to destroy another of your
> creations—me.
>
> Donna

"Donna, getting out emotions like that is just what
this group is for," June said. "How do you feel about
things now?"

"You heard the transformation during the letter,"
Donna said. "As I was ranting about my folks, all of a
sudden it hit me. God has always been there for me and

always will be, even if others aren't. It also got me thinking about how God views my parents. He loves them as much he loves me. He knows their shortcomings better than I do. He's a big God, and I'm a petty human wallowing in my own negativity. I need to seize his words and move on."

"Remember that, because there will be times when you find yourself slipping back into old ways of thinking," Sofia said.

While June asked Lisa to go next, Natalie thought about her own parents. She couldn't remember ever thinking about looking at them through God's eyes. She had been too self-absorbed.

Lisa began:

Dear God,

I have been so ashamed of my decision to have two abortions—to destroy your precious gift of life. If I knew then what I know now, my decisions would have been different. I grieve for my children, and I grieve for hurting your heart and spirit.

Please forgive my selfishness. I feel blessed to be redeemed and restored and to know that nothing can separate me from your love.

Please help me as I try to minister to other women about abortion. And please, Father, take care of my little ones until I can meet them face-to-face.

Lisa

"Thank you, Lisa," June said. "Is there anything you want to add?"

"No, I guess not."

"Tanika?"

"Here goes."

Dear Lord,

As David cried out to you in Psalm 51, "Have mercy on me, O God, according to your unfailing love; according to your great compassion blot out my transgression. Wash away all my iniquity and cleanse me from my sin ... Cleanse me with hyssop, and I will be clean; wash me, and I will be whiter than snow. Let me hear joy and gladness; let the bones you have crushed rejoice. Hide your face from my sins and blot out my iniquity. Create in me a pure heart, O God, and renew a steadfast spirit within me."

I have made this my prayer too, since I first acknowledged my sins of abortion and resentment toward Auntie Jo. Now, I thank you for forgiving me and for bringing back a light spirit to my heart. As you promise to do, you are turning my darkness into light.

I love you and praise your name.

Tanika

"Psalm 51 is an amazing example of repentance and forgiveness," June said. "It's another picture, much like the prodigal son, of God's love for those who turn and seek him. Thank you, Tanika. Very nice, everyone. It's obvious you put a lot of thought into your letters."

"Let's move on to our discussion for this evening," Sophia said. "I can't believe we have only a couple more weeks to go. Do you remember the first night of group when we talked about the symptoms of postabortion syndrome? A couple of those that we mentioned but haven't talked about in detail are depression and guilt. I don't think anyone ever totally escapes suffering from depression at some time or another. It's natural to feel depressed after key life experiences. Events such as the death of a loved one, divorce, loss of a dream, or health or financial problems can bring it on. I'm not talking about long-lasting clinical depression. I'm talking about situational depression that usually resolves itself within a reasonable period of time.

"The problem with depression after an abortion, or multiple abortions, is that it sometimes lingers for months and even years. Why?"

"I can't speak for the other ladies," Lisa said, "but I felt so isolated. Chuck didn't want to talk about it, and no one else knew. I didn't have anyone to talk to. At the time, it didn't occur to me to seek professional counseling because anyone associated with an abortion acted like it was no big deal. So, for me, when I couldn't talk things over with someone, all those yucky feelings had nowhere to go, and I turned inward. It was like a black cloud was hanging over my head."

"I know exactly what you mean, Lisa," Tanika said. "There's a hopelessness that takes over. You forget what it feels like to be happy. You forget what life felt like before the abortion."

"Liquor doesn't judge you," Donna said. "It's always there, always ready to listen, and always ready for a party."

Donna had a way of smiling a sad smile that always touched Natalie.

"In my case," she continued, "my depression led me to drinking, and my addiction fueled my depression."

"You've all touched on it," Sophia said. "When the 'yucky feelings,' as Lisa called them—emotions like anger, shame, guilt, and grief—aren't dealt with, we end up feeling sad, hopeless, and unable to enjoy life. That's when we overeat, sleep too much, drink too much, get angry at people, and the list goes on. These types of behaviors can destroy our lives and our relationships."

"One of those feelings is guilt," June said. "I have a theory about it. Several decades ago, marketers and psychologists decided it was bad to feel guilty about anything, so they got together and decided guilt isn't healthy. Look around. We have guilt-free foods, no-fault or guilt-free divorce, no-fault insurance, and so on. If it's not our fault, there's nothing to feel guilty about. As our letters have shown, several of us blamed others for a long time for the abortion, which helped us diminish those feelings of guilt. What we were denying is that guilt is a God-given emotion that makes us feel bad when we have committed a legal or moral offence. We are *supposed* to feel bad about it when we've done something wrong. Guilt is intended to make us sorry about our sins. At that point, we can repent, apologize, ask for forgiveness from God and from the person or persons we have offended.

"Our problems compound when we continue to feel guilty long after we have taken those steps of repenting, apologizing, and seeking forgiveness. It may last for weeks, months, or even years. It's false guilt and a form of self-punishment because we don't believe we deserve forgiveness. We become negative in our thoughts and actions. Our addictions may rage out of control, and the whole mess becomes a pattern even though, as we know through the Bible, we are forgiven. False guilt is a ploy by the enemy to keep you in a bondage of misery about your abortion.

"Listen as I read Proverbs 26:11. It paints a disgusting picture, but it pretty well describes what we do. 'As a dog returns to its vomit, so a fool repeats his folly.'"

It made sense to Natalie. She recognized in herself the tendency to return to old thought patterns and behaviors.

"Something else we want you to think about is whether your feeling is truly guilt or grief," June said. "Don't forget that society offers no way for you to grieve your child, or children, because our culture now believes that you haven't suffered a loss, only undergone a simple procedure. There's no body, no funeral, or no support of family and friends. Even the people who know what you've gone through may minimize the whole thing and encourage you to get on with your life. As a result, you bury those feelings and the need to grieve.

"Today in the Western world, it's almost as if our minds and emotions didn't exist before Sigmund Freud, but we know that God is our creator and the Great

121

Physician. He understands and cares about your psyche. Grief, like guilt, is God-given. It's a process, a series of feelings and steps designed to restore you to wholeness after a significant loss. Isn't this a huge part of why we all came to a group like this? In our normal lives, this process wasn't able to take place. If nothing else, Sofia and I hope that through this group you are realizing the importance of grieving your lost children."

Sofia said, "Go to Isaiah 61:1–3 in your Bibles. Let's read it together."

Natalie and the others turned to the verse in their Bibles. Sofia led them in reading, "'The Spirit of the Sovereign Lord is on me, because the Lord has anointed me to preach good news to the poor. He has sent me to bind up the brokenhearted, to proclaim freedom to the captives, and release from darkness for the prisoners; to proclaim the year of the Lord's favor and the day of vengeance of our God, to comfort all who mourn, and provide for those who grieve in Zion—to bestow on them a crown of beauty instead of ashes, the oil of gladness instead of mourning, and a garment of praise instead of a spirit of despair. They will be called oaks of righteousness, a planting of the Lord for the display of his splendor.'"

"Here's another good verse for us: 'Rejoice with those who rejoice and weep with those who weep' (Romans 12:15)."

"That's why we're here," Sophia said. "You are not alone."

"Tonight, we're talking about grief," Jane said. "Your assignment for next week is twofold. We want you to write a letter to your baby, or babies, expressing what you would like to say to them, if you could. Secondly, we want you to come up with a way to memorialize your baby or babies. Use your imagination and creativity on this. Some people plant a tree in honor of their babies; others write a poem or a song or draw a picture. Some people put mementos in a box for their babies, like family pictures.

"This assignment will be easier if you know something about your baby. What I mean is, perhaps you already have a sense of the sex of your baby, and perhaps you have already named your baby. If not, ask God to show you. In Jeremiah 33:3, it says, 'Call to me and I will answer you and tell you great and unsearchable things you do not know.' And God will show you. We don't want you to feel pressured that this week you have to figure out the baby's sex and name him or her, but we don't want you to avoid thinking and praying about it either. Having an idea about these things is valuable to the process of humanizing your baby and bringing closure to the grieving process."

Natalie looked around. There was a steely silence as the others, she presumed, were as overwhelmed as she was at the idea of trying to know her baby.

June asked Sofia if she would like to share her letters and memorial.

"When I got to where you are in this group," Sofia said, "I had never thought about names or genders of my babies. So, as I prepared to write my letters, I prayed to God to show me what I needed to know in order to fulfill this assignment and to embrace the grief that I had shoved down inside. God was faithful in answering that prayer for me, and I know he will do the same thing for you.

"We will all know when we get to heaven, but for us still here on earth, it helps to give our children an identity.

If you lost a child as an infant, I'm sure you would imagine what they would have looked like and what talents and hobbies they would have enjoyed. It's the same thing.

"I had the distinct feeling that I had a son and a daughter, so I wrote two letters. They are very similar except for the sections about their fathers. I'll read the one to my daughter."

Right off, Sofia's voice shook with emotion.

Dear Amy,

My beautiful daughter. I am so sorry I aborted you. Please forgive me. Words are inadequate to express my feelings of regret and sadness. It is only through Christ that I have learned to forgive myself and your dad, and to allow myself to acknowledge you as a baby and not a blob of tissue. It has been just a few months since I first allowed myself to think of you and to mourn you. Now, there isn't a day that goes by that I don't think of you.

It was painful to Natalie to hear the emotion in Sofia's voice as she read her letter to her daughter, Amy, aborted more than a decade ago. Natalie felt miserable as Sofia continued through muffled sobs. *How will I ever be able to write and then read my own letter?*

I know you have blue eyes and brown hair. Your half brother is there with you in heaven. I have to admit that, at times,

I have yearned for Jesus to call me home
so I can be with you both. The passage
of time is bittersweet. I know each year
brings me closer to heaven, but with each
year, I miss you and your brother more
and more. It helps to know you are in
the loving care of our Lord Jesus Christ.
What a wonderful reunion we will have
on my homecoming day!

At this point, Sofia reached for a tissue. "Sorry," she
said as she dabbed at her nose. "This never gets easier.
I'm almost done."

I pray for your dad's salvation, but know
that this, too, must be left in the Lord's
hands. I will always consider your dad
the love of my life. He is so intelligent and
handsome, but he never learned to cherish
life and love. Oh, how I wish things could
have been different for all of us.

Even though I know heaven is wonderful
beyond my understanding, I find myself
hoping that you're happy and that you can
forgive me. Until we meet again, I want
you to know that I don't want your death
and your brother's death to be in vain. As
long as I am on earth, I will speak and act
against the horror of abortion.

Love,
Mom

Sofia took a deep breath. "Here," she said, "is my memorial."

She opened a small cedar box to reveal two miniature dolls. One was covered in a small piece of pink flannel, and the other one was covered in blue. She included pictures of herself with each of the baby's fathers. Each baby also had its own miniature stuffed animal.

"I'll pass it around so you can take a look," Sofia said.

"This is so sweet," Tanika said. "It gives me a good idea of what I'd like to do."

"Nice," Donna said.

When it came around to her, Natalie touched the babies and looked at the photos of a young Sofia standing next to a guy with long blond hair in one, and sitting on the lap of a different guy in the other photo. Looking at the pictures and the box made Natalie feel like she was intruding on something very personal.

"Thank you for sharing," Natalie said.

After Lisa had a chance to look in the box, June began to read her letter:

Dear Son,

I named you Timmy. I imagine you running in a green field with your blond curls blowing in a gentle breeze. I imagine your laugh as a toddler and your curiosity as you grab for a puppy's tail. I imagine you doing all the things and leaning all the things we take for granted with our children every day, only I imagine you doing these things in heaven. I imagine the wonderful big brother you would have been to Ben and Emily. I imagine your life as an adult and what you might have become. I imagine you as a dad with children of your own and how happy you would have been. I think of you and miss you every day. Please forgive me for not choosing *you*.

Love,
Mommy

June didn't display the same outward emotion that Sofia did, but Natalie was touched by this sweet letter about a son June had never known. Natalie felt a tear run down her cheek. June passed around a picture of a tree that stood about twelve feet tall.

"This is a tree my husband helped me plant in memory of Timmy," June explained. "I can see it when I look out my kitchen window. I watch it change with the seasons, and it helps me remember him. It's a comfort. When I am long gone, I know the tree will remain. It's a poor substitute for a child, but I view it as a type of legacy."

June looked at everyone around the room.

"We don't expect you to do the same things we have done, not unless you want to. This week will be about you identifying your child, or children, and memorializing them in a way that is meaningful to you. However, the letters are more important, and we ask that you write those, regardless of what else you do. If you can't think of a memorial, it's not a problem. Down the road, the perfect thing may come to you, and you can do it then in memory of your child. Does anyone have any questions?"

Everyone was silent. Natalie assumed they were all thinking the same thing she was, *This is overwhelming and beyond what I can do.* She had never even had the courage to utter the word "abortion" until this group, let alone dwell on details of the little life she had destroyed.

"We recognize this will be a difficult week for you," Sofia said, "and we will be praying for you. Please feel free to call either of us if you want to."

"I'll close in prayer," June said. "Heavenly Father, we thank you for who you are. We thank you that you are caring for our children in heaven and that you are caring for us in our grief. Please be with these women this week as they seek you. As they write to their children and prepare a memorial of some kind, make this week an exercise in the celebration of life as much as a commemoration of death. In your son's name. Amen."

The women hugged one another and filed silently out of the room.

Natalie burst into tears when she got to her car. *This is going to be a difficult week.*

CHAPTER 8

Healing

> He will wipe away every tear from their
> eyes. There will be no more death or
> mourning or crying or pain, for the
> old order of things has passed away.
> —Revelation 21:4

Group—Week Seven

"Hi, ladies. How was your week?"

"Well, Sofia, it was difficult," Donna said.

Natalie thought Donna sounded mad. It *had* been a difficult week. After telling Randy the truth last week and writing her letter this week, she couldn't remember when she had felt so exhausted emotionally, at least not since the abortion. The best part was how Randy had held her after she showed him her letter. He was being supportive, just as he had promised.

"Natalie, how about you?"

"I had a tough time writing my letter, but it was a valuable experience," she said.

"Did everyone complete their letters and memorials?" Sofia asked.

Natalie noticed everyone nodding nervously. No one wanted to be the first to share her letter.

"Before we get started, let's pray," Sofia said. "Lord, June and I know seeking healing from our abortions has not been an easy journey for us or for the participants gathered here this evening, but you are the Great Sustainer. One of my favorite verses, Isaiah 40:31, says, 'But those who hope in the Lord will renew their strength. They will soar on wings like eagles; they will run and not grow weary, they will walk and not grow faint.' So, tonight I pray for renewed strength for Donna, and Natalie, and Tanika, and Lisa. We seek your presence tonight and always. In Jesus's name. Amen."

"Who would like to read her letter first?" Jane asked.

"I will," Tanika answered.

Dear Rodney,

You may not have been conceived in love, but you are mourned and remembered in love. Please forgive my great-aunt for insisting on the abortion and me for letting it happen. Great-Auntie Jo had her reasons for believing it was the best choice, and I was scared and still a baby myself. I was too young and stupid to know how to stand up for you.

You have a half brother and a half sister who would have loved to have had a big brother to play ball with and hang out with. Someday I will tell them about you and explain why taking a life, regardless of the circumstances, is never the best choice.

Please know that I wanted you and that I love you.

Mom

Natalie clenched her teeth while listening to Tanika's letter. *Oh God, help me get through tonight. This is gut-wrenching.* She grabbed a tissue and watched as Tanika remained dry-eyed and calmly pulled out a shoebox covered in pale blue paper.

"This is my memorial," she said.

She removed the lid to reveal a small stuffed bunny with a blue bow tie and, nestled beside it, a miniature black baby doll dressed in a blue sleeper.

"I also put in a picture of myself when I was fifteen, and a picture of me and my kids now.

"Can you pass that around?" Lisa asked. "I'd like to see it."

"Sure."

"How did you feel about writing your letter?" Sofia asked.

"It was fine," Tanika said. "I really thought I would be more upset than I was. I had a good time putting the box together, and I'll keep the letter with the box. When the time comes to tell my kids, I'll show them this. I'm glad I did it."

"Thank you, Tanika. It's beautiful," June said. "Who's next?"

"I'll go," Donna said. "Wow. I don't know if I can get through this."

"Take your time."

Donna cleared her throat and motioned for Natalie to pass the box of tissues. With her letter in one hand and a tissue in the other, Donna began.

> Dear Dougie,
>
> I look back at the decisions I have made in my life and am ashamed at how many of them were bad decisions. The worst decision I have ever made was to end your life. I wish I could turn back the clock and do things over, but I can't.

At this point, Donna bowed her head and was silent for a few seconds while she composed herself. Natalie touched her shoulder, just as a gesture of support, and could feel her shaking. Donna straightened up in her chair and continued.

> Instead, now I am trying to make good decisions with my life and live in a way that would make you proud of me. I named you Douglas Gregory for my dad and your dad. When I think about

you, I see a tall young man with dark, bushy hair and deep brown eyes. I see you laughing and talking with the angels. I imagine you with your arms outstretched, praising God.

I am so thankful there is a heaven and that your father and I will be reunited with you. On that day, I pray that I will hear you say that you forgive me. I love you, my unborn child.

Mommy

"My memorial isn't quite finished, but it will be soon," Donna said.

From her bag, she pulled out a cross-stitch sampler. It had the alphabet across the top like old samplers Natalie had seen, but at the bottom was a cross-stitched crib. Above the crib, Donna was stitching the name Douglas Gregory.

"The pattern has a place for date of birth, but obviously that doesn't apply. I'm going to put a couple of angels there instead."

Donna held up the piece and indicated where the angels would be.

"How long have you been working on this?" Natalie asked. She was impressed with how beautiful it was and how much work must have already gone into it.

"I started this even before I came to group," Donna said. "I didn't know if I would complete it or what I would do with it, so when we got our assignment last week, the purpose for it became clear."

"What are you going to do with it when you're finished?" Sofia asked.

"I've thought a lot about that," Donna said. "At first, I didn't think I wanted anyone to see it, but now, I plan to frame it and put it in my bedroom. If someone wants to ask me about it, I'll tell them. It will be quite the icebreaker, especially with my family."

"That's bold," Tanika said.

"You can say that again," Natalie added. "Good for you."

Sofia examined the fabric and stitching. "How long have you cross-stitched, Donna? This is beautiful work."

"I picked it up in one of my many visits to rehab. I enjoy it. It's a soothing pastime."

"Very nice. Natalie or Lisa, who wants to be next?"

I don't ever want to do this, Natalie thought to herself. She and Lisa exchanged glances.

Natalie smiled and said, "Lisa can go next, if that's okay with her."

Everyone chuckled, and Lisa said she didn't mind at all. She found her letter and began:

Dear Children,

Please forgive me for my selfish decision to abort you. The lifelong consequences of those decisions didn't occur to me at the time. I let myself be deceived by the idea that you were a problem to be dispensed with. At the time, I didn't think about the people you were created to be. When I destroyed you, I played God. Your father and I now know and acknowledge our sin before God and are aware that our lives move forward only by virtue of His forgiveness and mercy.

One of those lifelong consequences is that now that our other children are married and gone, I know how empty a house can be. You see, as I am writing this letter, you kids would still be here with us. I miss you and love you both.

Mom

Lisa sighed. "I was very nervous thinking about sexes and names and finally resolved not to worry about it. That's when I wrote my letter. Then, the next night, I had a dream, and I tried to draw what I saw in my dream. I still don't have names, but that may come down the road."

With that, Lisa reached under the table and pulled out a framed charcoal drawing. Natalie thought it displayed real talent. There was an ethereal quality about it that was difficult to describe. The lower third of the picture depicted two in utero babies. The next tier showed two young children, a girl and a boy, looking with wonder at a flower they held jointly by the stem. At the top of the drawing were the faces of two young adults, reminiscent of graduation pictures.

"I took some drawing classes years ago but hadn't done anything in a while. I am pleased with the way it turned out."

"You did that in less than a week?" June asked.

"I did it in two or three hours. I was inspired."

"We have some talent in this room!" Tanika said. "That's beautiful."

"Too bad I didn't get any of it!" Natalie joked. Now that she had seen everyone's memorial, she felt badly that she hadn't felt compelled to prepare one. She couldn't draw or sew, and she didn't care for the idea of putting a doll in a box. She had thought about planting a tree or having a stepping-stone engraved for the garden, but nothing seemed right. Natalie realized Lisa was talking. She was saying that, like Donna, she planned to hang the picture in her bedroom.

"If my husband doesn't object, that's where it will go. If he does, I'll find someplace else to hang it, but I am going to put it up." Lisa, who had made her presentation without a sniffle, began to cry.

"I'm sorry, but sometimes the reality of what we did really gets to me. Thank God for his forgiveness. Thank God for this group. And thank God for the two of you, June and Sofia. It can't be easy to come here every week to help us and to relive your own experiences."

June smiled. "It's a privilege for us to be part of this, to come here and watch God at work," she said. "We just show up, but thank you."

Sofia looked at Natalie. "Okay, it's your turn."

"Well, it's intimidating to go after all your beautiful memorials. I haven't done one yet. I'm not gifted in the area of crafts. I'm still praying about what I want to do. Randy and I talked about planting a tree, but we haven't decided yet."

"It's okay, Natalie," Sofia said. "You don't have to do anything at all if you don't want to. And there's no time limit on this. Maybe you'll think of something later. If you do a memorial, do it because it's meaningful to you, not because you think you must. You did write a letter, though, right?"

"Yes, but that's another thing. I really don't know the sex or name of the baby. I ..."

"It's okay, Natalie. You'll know when you get to heaven."

"All right, here's my letter."

Dear Baby,

I don't know if you are a girl or a boy. All I know is that I made a terrible mistake that day when I went into the abortion clinic. They assured me I would feel relieved. They assured me it was the best decision I could make. They told me my life would go on without interruption.

I wanted to believe everything they said. Well, I did feel relieved at first, but that changed quickly. My life didn't go on without interruption, and certainly, neither did yours. It was the worst decision I could have made for both of us.

I felt so deceived after I aborted you. For a long time, I blamed others, but ultimately it was my decision. I am sorry for the mistake I made that cost you your life and our life together. Please forgive me.

Love, Your mother

"That's a beautiful letter, Natalie," Sofia said.

"I cried for hours the evening I wrote this letter. It was like my first night here in group. I was mourning. Plus, now that he knows, Randy is mourning with me. When you allow yourself to think about it, it becomes apparent how far-reaching the consequences are for taking a little life. Someone said it a couple of weeks ago: 'Abortion never goes away.' The so-called quick fix and easy solution never go away."

"Thank you all for sharing your letters," June said. "We have something else for you to do tonight. It will also be difficult, but it has to do with the concept of closure. We are going to go outside in a few minutes and have a balloon release. There are helium balloons for each of you, one for each baby you aborted. Releasing them symbolizes releasing your children to their heavenly Father. Sofia has the balloons ready for you in the hallway."

Natalie wasn't sure she had heard correctly. She looked around the room, and Donna and Tanika had bewildered looks on their faces too. She took her lead from Lisa, who stood up and led the others out of the room.

Sofia handed Natalie, Donna, and Tanika one balloon each. Lisa received two. When the ladies got outside, Sofia prayed a brief prayer aloud, asking for peace for the women as they released their children to God.

June told them they could take their time and release their balloons when they were ready. Natalie was overwhelmed. She had spent the last week trying to connect to her child, and now she was letting go. *Letting go.* She didn't want to.

June and Sofia observed the women as they spread out in the parking lot and stood with the balloons. Donna was the first to let go of the string. After just a few moments, she was smiling as she walked back to where June and Sofia were standing. In a whisper, she said, "That was wonderful. Thank you."

The three of them watched Donna's balloon and waited on the other women to release theirs. Next, Tanika stood perfectly still while her balloon ascended. When it was out of sight, she walked over to June, Sofia, and Donna and hugged each woman.

Lisa held a balloon in each hand, her eyes closed and her lips moving in silent prayer. Suddenly, she lifted her arms above her head and let go of both balloons at the same time. Her arms remained in the air in praise. "Thank you, Jesus," she said over and over as she watched the balloons rise. The balloons stayed close together and looked as if they were touching when they finally disappeared from sight.

Sofia had been watching Natalie as she walked around in a small circle, still grasping her balloon.

Tears were streaming down Natalie's face as she looked up when Sofia approached her. Natalie hugged Sofia and sobbed.

"It's okay, Natalie. I know it's hard. You come to this workshop, and for the first time ever, you're encouraged to talk and think about your child. Now we're asking you to give up that child and release it back to the Lord."

"That's just it. I don't want to. I know I have to, but if I let this go, I won't have anything left. Nothing."

"You know that's not true. For the first time, you've acknowledged your child in this world. Now you have a whole new way to remember and speak about your baby. Releasing this balloon is symbolic of something you have already known, that your baby is safe in heaven. If you want me to, I'll stand here with you while you release the balloon."

"Okay."

Sofia stood with her arm around Natalie's shoulder. Natalie looked behind her to see the other four women standing arm in arm about ten feet behind her, each with her head bowed, praying.

"Bye, baby," Natalie whispered as she released her hold on the balloon. Everyone was quiet as they went back inside. June and Sofia shared a glance and then looked at the women.

"We know this has been an emotional evening for you, and we're going to close in just a minute," June said. "Please remember that next week is our final week together until the reunion, so please plan to be here."

June bowed her head and was starting to pray when Donna said, "Excuse me, June, but there's something I need to tell the group."

"Please, go ahead, Donna."

"Well, as you remember, when we entered this workshop, we agreed to come to these meetings sober. Don't worry, I'm sober, but I wanted you to know that this week I was really tempted to drink, more so than at any other time in the past several months. I was home alone, as usual, and it was all I could do to keep from going to the carryout on the corner and getting a six-pack. For a while, I actually sat on my hands so I couldn't pick up my keys."

"What kept you from it?" June asked.

"Well, a couple of things. First of all, when I realized I was in serious trouble, I called my therapist. We talked for a while, and it really helped, but there was something missing. When I got off the phone, I opened my Bible, and that verse out of 1 Peter came to me. The one about Satan being a prowling lion looking for whom he can devour. At that moment, the Lord spoke to me, and I realized how important this group is. As I have said before, this single issue—my abortion—is the common source of all my other problems. The reason I'm telling you this is because I realize how much the evil one wants me and each of you to remain in bondage to our past. He doesn't want us here in the first place, but if he can keep us from getting anything out of it, the victory is his, not ours. Plus, I thought of each of you, and I didn't want to let you down."

"Thank you for sharing that with us, Donna. There is something special about the group dynamic. We would have been concerned about you, not let down. We're in this together. I'm thankful your therapist was available, and I'm thankful you had scripture to remind you that we are all targets for the enemy. Your experience is an example to us all to stay in the Word and close to the Lord. Let's pray.

"Father, this has been an emotional evening for all of us, and our hearts are full. We take comfort in knowing our little ones are safe with you. Thank you for your protection of our sister Donna. Be with us as we prepare to end our time together on Thursday evenings. Help us speak what should yet be spoken, and help us hear what should yet be heard. It is in your son's name we pray. Amen."

CHAPTER 9

Restoration

He restores my soul.
—Psalm 23:3

Group—Week Eight

*N*atalie couldn't believe this was the final night of group. She was not the same person who entered this building seven Thursdays ago. She had lied to her husband about where she was going, and when she arrived, she argued with herself about entering the room. Once inside, she was overwhelmed with the idea of talking with strangers about the worst thing that had ever happened to her. Tonight, she had the support of a loving husband and called those strangers friends. She was going to miss the weekly support of these loving women—the only ones who could fully understand the invisible wounds left from her abortion experience.

The meeting room had been transformed. The lights were dimmed, and an altar had been set up at the front of the room. On the altar stood a cross and a candle. Music was playing softly in the background. Where the tables had been, there was a row of chairs for the participants and leaders. The easel with the flip chart from the first night of group was also placed up front. On it was the list of things each member wanted to accomplish during their time together. As Natalie was studying it, June greeted her.

"This is a special evening, Natalie. I'm so proud of you for sticking with us. I know at times it was difficult for you."

"You're right, but you and Sofia provided the support I needed to see it through. We all owe you both so much."

"Thank you, Natalie, but you don't owe us anything. It's a way for us to give back. Remember, there were others here for us when we went through our groups."

"I'll always remember you," Natalie said.

June looked Natalie in the eye and said, "Even though I have led many women through this program, I have a feeling I'll always remember you too. You're my only pickleball player ever!"

They hugged, then Natalie turned to join the other women who were already seated. She could tell the ladies were as keyed up about the memorial service as she was. Sofia got up from her chair and stood in front of them.

"Thank you for being here tonight. I have enjoyed getting to know you. You are an amazing group of ladies who worked very hard these past weeks. Look at our flip chart and consider the goals you have achieved. This may be the end of our time together, but it is a new beginning for you and your healing journey. Tonight, we will talk about where you go from here, and, of course, we will memorialize your children. They are worthy of being honored and remembered.

"Let's open by standing and praying the Lord's Prayer. Our Father in heaven, hallowed be your name, your kingdom come, your will be done on earth as it is in heaven. Give us this day our daily bread. Forgive us our debts as we forgive our debtors. And lead us not into temptation, but deliver us from evil, for yours is the kingdom and the power and the glory forever. Amen."

The Lord's Prayer ... how beautiful, Natalie thought. She loved hearing it sung and couldn't recite it without hearing the music in her head.

"And now, June wants to share her thoughts with you."

June stepped to the front of the room.

"Sophia and I are so proud of you, but as we transition out of our weekly meetings, I want to caution you that you will be tempted to fall back into old ways of thinking about your lives. You will be tempted to believe, once again, that you are not forgiven for your abortions and that this group was a futile exercise. Do not believe the lies of the enemy.

"When a child is learning to walk and they fall down, they don't go back to crawling. They get up and walk again. If, from time-to-time, your emotions and thoughts stumble, remember that Jesus died on the cross for you. But, he no longer hangs there. He is alive in you, and you in Him. It says in 2 Corinthians 5:17, 'Therefore, if anyone is in Christ, he is a new creation; the old is gone, the new has come!' You, ladies, are new creations in Christ. Don't let anyone steal that from you."

Natalie liked the idea of being a new creation. Since the group, the burden of her secret had been lifted from her, and her marriage was becoming a new creation based on truth. Her old life was gone.

June returned to her seat, and Sofia handed out the words to a song called "At the Cross." Natalie wasn't familiar with it, but she could tell by the words it was powerful. Natalie and the others all looked surprised when Sofia brought out a guitar.

Sofia played through the tune and then led them in the song:

> I know a place,
> A wonderful place,
> Where accused and condemned
> Find mercy and grace.
>
> Where the wrongs we have done,
> And the wrongs done to us
> Were nailed there with Him,
> There on the cross.
>
> At the cross,
> He died for our sins.
> At the cross, He gave us life again.

By the time they sang the verse and chorus twice, everyone was crying. June passed around tissues after she grabbed one for herself.

At the close of the song, June joined Sofia at the front.

146

"Thank you, Sofia. That was beautiful. Tonight is a celebration of the completion of our workshop, but it is also a special time to acknowledge and celebrate our children.

"When we call your name, please come forward. We will give each of you a candle to light in memory of each of your babies. You are going to light them from the big candle, which represents Jesus. Then you can stand them up in the holders we have on the table. If you would like to say something before you light your candle, or simply state the name of your child, we encourage you to do so. We also have a little something for each of you. When you're finished lighting your candles, you may return to your seat until everyone is finished.

"Lisa."

All eyes were on Lisa as she stood and walked forward. June positioned Lisa between her and Sofia, facing the other women.

"Lisa," Sofia began, "we thank you for being part of this group. We thank God for your maturity as a Christian and for your desire to serve others through your experiences. You are God's beloved daughter, and the verse we have chosen for your bookmark is Proverbs 31:26: 'She speaks with Wisdom and faithful instruction is on her tongue.'"

Natalie noticed blue and pink pieces of paper in June's hand.

"Lisa," June said, "these are Certificates of Dedication for your children. You know you have a girl and a boy, and you may fill in the names later, if you would like. We are handing you two candles to light for your children. When you have lit them and placed them in the holders, take a rose for each child. Is there anything you would like to say to the group?"

"Yes," Lisa said in a whisper.

She sniffled and cleared her throat.

"First of all, I want to thank both of you, June and Sofia, and I want to thank Tanika, Donna, and Natalie. I've come to know each of you as sisters in Christ, and I love each of you. Thank you for allowing me to give life to my children and to grieve their deaths."

Lisa started to turn to the altar and then turned back. "One more thing. I know not all of you share my desire to talk about your abortions publicly, but I just want to encourage you. By opening up to others, you may be helping someone else more than you'll ever know. I hope that you'll each pray about it. Each of us here has been given a gift through this group, and there are so many women like we were—in isolation and in pain about their abortions."

Lisa went to the altar and lit each of her candles. She placed them carefully in holders and selected two red roses. As she returned to her seat, June called Donna's name.

"Donna, we love you. There were times when we despaired of your getting through group. I have to admit I was fearful that your addiction might overtake you again. Forgive me. I shouldn't have doubted you, and I shouldn't have doubted the Lord. You are a picture of perseverance and faithfulness. The verse we selected for your bookmark is from Matthew 12:20, based on Isaiah 42:3. It says, 'A bruised reed he will not break, and a smoldering wick he will not snuff out, till he leads justice to victory.'"

"Thank you," Donna said.

"Donna," Sofia said, "here is your Certificate of Dedication for Douglas Gregory and your candle. Once you light your candle, don't forget to take your rose. Is there anything you would like to say to the group?"

"I don't think I can." Donna laughed and sobbed at the same time. "Just … thank you."

Donna lit her candle, picked up her rose, and sat down.

"Tanika, please come forward," Sofia said. "All of you have worked hard in this group, but none of you has worked any harder than this young lady. We are so glad you came to group and thank God for the grace and forgiveness he has brought into your life. I don't think we saw you crack a smile the first three or four weeks of group. And now look at you!"

Tanika smiled broadly. "Don't make me cry," she said.

"We'll try not to! On your bookmark, we placed Psalm 147:3: 'He heals the brokenhearted and binds up their wounds.'"

"Amen," Tanika said.

"Tanika," June said, "here is your Certificate of Dedication for Rodney and your candle. Is there anything you would like to say?"

"Well, just that I really loved my great-aunt, and I thank this group for helping me forgive her. When I light my candle, I'm also remembering her because I really believe she's with my baby in heaven."

149

To this point, Natalie had only sniffled through the presentations, but now she started crying. She watched as Tanika lit her candle and took her rose. She knew she would be next and was resigned to finishing the group as she had begun—a blubbering mess.

"Miss Natalie," June said. "Bring your tissues and come up here. It's okay. Remember the handout Sofia gave you about tears? They are healing. Just think about how far the Lord has brought you since those first weeks when you were supposedly playing pickleball! And he's not finished with you. On your bookmark is Philippians 1:6. 'Being confident of this, that he who began a good work in you will carry it out on to completion until the day of Christ Jesus.'"

Natalie looked at the beautiful handmade bookmark and cried. She tried to smile but nodded instead.

"Natalie, here is your Certificate of Dedication for your baby," Sofia said. "It's on yellow for now. If you discern whether it was a girl or a boy, let us know, and we'll redo this for you. Now, here is your candle. Is there anything you would like to say?"

"Words ... aren't ... adequate," Natalie stammered amid sobs. "Changed my life ... and ... my marriage. Thank you."

Natalie went to the altar and lit her candle in spite of her hand shaking nervously. As she placed the candle in the holder, she distinctly heard the name "Abigail." Abigail. It was the confirmation she had prayed for. Her child had been a daughter. *This is for you, my dear Abigail.* Natalie took her rose and returned to her seat.

"Ladies," Sofia said, "at the conclusion of the service,

we are going to have refreshments, but before we close, we want to sing 'Amazing Grace.' Let's join hands."

They formed a circle between the chairs and the altar, and Sofia started the song they all knew so well:

> Amazing Grace! How sweet the sound
> That saved a wretch like me!
> I once was lost, but now am found
> Was blind, but now I see
> 'Twas grace that taught my heart to fear
> And grace my fears relieved;
> How precious did that grace appear
> The hour I first believed!
>
> Through many dangers, toils and snares,
> I have already come;
> 'Tis grace hath brought me safe thus far,
> And grace will lead me home.
>
> When we've been there ten–thousand years,
> Bright shining as the sun,
> We've no less days to sing God's praise
> Than when we'd first begun.

At the close of the song, they stood quietly. Natalie silently thanked him for revealing her baby's gender and name. Following the service, they had refreshments and laughed together as they had the past seven weeks, but tonight was different. No one voiced the fear, but Natalie felt it. She was nervous about leaving the group, yet she knew it was time. She was putting her past in its proper place and moving forward, just like the other ladies.

Her life had already begun to change, and for that she was grateful. She would continue to mature in her new, healthy relationship with the Lord and with her husband. The group had served its purpose.

CHAPTER 10

Reunion

For I know the thoughts I think
toward you, says the Lord, thoughts
of peace, and not of evil, to give
you a future and a hope.
—Jeremiah 29:11 NKJ

Donna's House—Six Weeks Later

As planned, June and Sofia saw the women again six weeks after the memorial service. Everyone prepared a dish and met at Donna's apartment.

After they all hugged and said how much they had missed one another, Donna encouraged them to look at her family pictures that dotted the hallway toward her bedroom.

"I just put these up. They help me remember they're

153

only people and not some evil spirits I've conjured up in my mind."

Donna chuckled, and Natalie remembered how much she had enjoyed Donna during group.

"Plus, I wanted you to see the crazy people I talked about for eight weeks," she added.

Natalie admired a picture of remarkably young-looking parents seated on a sofa encircled by five adult children. Next to it was a similarly situated picture with two kids encircled by five babies, approximately six months to six years old. Natalie thought about the poor parenting Donna had experienced. Her youthful parents were probably too tired and overwhelmed to always make good decisions. Then she spotted Donna's high school graduation picture. What a beautiful girl Donna had been. She was much older now, but the brightness in her eyes remained. *Thank you, Lord*, Natalie prayed silently, *for delivering Donna from alcoholism and for continuing to repair the relationships in her family. Thank you for bringing Donna to our group and for the healing she received there.*

As Donna showed them through the rest of the modest apartment and they passed her bedroom, Natalie noticed the framed needlepoint on the wall.

"There it is!" Natalie said. "You finished Dougie's cross-stitch. It's beautiful."

Donna beamed. "Thank you. I'm so glad I have it."

Everyone gathered around to admire the completed sampler with Douglas Gregory's name on it.

The six of them headed for the kitchen, filled their plates, and crowded around a dinette table better suited for four.

"Before we dig in, I'd like to say the blessing," Donna said. "Holy Father, we are thankful for this gathering. Thank you for your loving kindness in bringing us together for group and together again tonight. We thank you for June and Sofia, who opened up their lives to us. Thank you for your grace and mercy that even while we were walking away from you, you waited for us with open arms. Thank you for allowing us to acknowledge and grieve our lost children. We thank you for changed lives as a result of our group. But as happy as we are, we also remember Meredith, who is missing from this celebration. I've thought of her so often, Lord. We pray for her healing, too, and that people in her life will help draw her closer to you. Be with us and guide us as we move forward. Now we ask you to bless this food and our lives. In the name of Jesus, amen."

After small talk about families and jobs, June asked everyone what they thought about the group since there had been time to reflect on the experience.

"As far as I'm concerned, other than reading the Bible, it was the best thing I've done since I became a Christian," Lisa said. "I can live with myself again, and Chuck and I continue to grow closer. Because we have talked about this issue, we are able to talk about other things now too. It was a wonderful program, and I'm thankful for it every day. The bad thing is I miss you ladies!"

"I miss you too," Tanika said. "It was so refreshing to be able to speak openly about my abortion without fear of judgment. A load has been lifted from my mind about the baby. It's so true about feelings following the actions.

I'm determined to release Auntie Jo, for as much my sake as hers, and it's happening."

"That's wonderful," Sofia said.

"There's just one thing I wasn't prepared for."

"What's that?"

"Thursday nights just aren't the same!"

"That's the truth!" Natalie said.

"I can tell you what I thought of group," Donna said. *"It saved my life."*

"What do you mean?" June asked.

"I mean it literally saved my life. If this group hadn't been there for me, I don't think I would have made it. God revealed to me that my abortion was my underlying problem, but I didn't know what to do about it. You ladies were Jesus to me. You ministered to me. You saved my life."

Sofia and June were speechless. Donna popped up from her seat and bear-hugged June first, then Sofia, then everyone else.

"Hey, this is supposed to be a happy occasion," Tanika said, half laughing and half crying.

Natalie used her napkin for a tissue.

"How's your pickleball game these days?" Tanika asked Natalie with a broad smile.

"Now that I'm really playing instead of lying about it, it's pretty good," Natalie said.

They all smiled, and Natalie knew they were waiting for her to say something about how she had been doing the past six weeks. She remembered how scared she had been the first night of group. Now she was no longer reluctant to share what was on her heart.

"I've been waiting to tell all of you that during our memorial service, the name Abigail came to me, and I felt like God was telling me my baby had been a little girl."

"I love the name Abigail," Sofia said.

"Me too," Lisa said.

"Also," Natalie continued, "remember how I didn't know what I wanted to do for a memorial? Well, here it is," she said as she stuck out her right hand. "It's a mother's ring with a birthstone for what would have been my baby's birth month."

"Oh, Natalie, that's beautiful," June said. "What are you going to say when someone asks you about it?"

"I'll just say it's for my baby who's in heaven. Maybe it will start a conversation about why, and I'll tell the truth. But that's not all. There's room for the new baby's birthstone too. We're pregnant."

Donna shrieked, "Natalie, that's terrific!"

Several of them said congratulations all at once. June leaned over and hugged her.

"Oh, sweetie, I'm so happy for you and Randy."

Natalie was happy too. For the first time since her abortion, Natalie was truly, completely happy.

ENDNOTES

Chapter 2

Teri I. Reisser and Paul C. Reisser, *A Solitary Sorrow* (Colorado Springs: Waterbrook Press, 1999), 45–49.

Chapter 3

Jack W. Hayford, Spirit Filled Life Bible "Tears and Brokenness in Victorious Warfare, Faith's Warfare" (Nashville: Thomas Nelson Publishers, 1991), 185.

Chapter 9

The Lord's Prayer (Matthew 6:9–13).
"At the Cross," Randy Butler and Terry Butler (Mercy/ Vineyard Publishing, 1993) (ASCAP). Print license #424972.

John Newton, "Amazing Grace," in *Olney Hymns* (London: W. Oliver, 1779).

Chapter 10

Jeremiah 29:11 taken from the New King James Version. Copyright 1982 by Thomas Nelson. Used by permission. All rights reserved.

RESOURCES

Healing Workshops

Many different postabortion healing workshops are available. There is no age limit to participation. Most groups are multigenerational, although there are workshops designed specifically for teens. Other groups may be virtual or one-on-one, and there are also groups for men. If you prefer a nonfaith-based approach, there's a group for you. Call Support After Abortion at 1-844-289-HOPE. They will connect you with caring, nonjudgmental postabortion help in your area.

Support After Abortion
www.supportafterabortion.com
1-844-289-HOPE (4673)

Abortion Pill Reversal

In the story you have just read, Meredith chose to have an abortion procedure known as a medical termination, RU-486, or the abortion pill. The patient is required to take two different medications, first mifepristone, followed by misoprostol thirty-six to forty-eight hours later. Often, a woman will regret this decision after the first dose of medicine. There is now a time-sensitive procedure called *abortion pill reversal* that may save the pregnancy *if initiated prior* to the second dose of medicine. Call the number below for more information and to be referred immediately to a health care professional in your area:

Abortion Pill Reversal
24/7 Helpline: 1-877-558-0333

What About God?

Each woman in this story was a Christian. This belief, and ongoing study of the Bible, helped them to understand the depth of God's love, which led to healing, forgiveness, and a new way of dealing with their pasts.

Do you believe?

Becoming a follower of Jesus Christ (a Christian) is more than living a certain way, participating in church services, or praying a particular prayer. What you need to know is that Jesus Christ loves you and died on the cross to save you from your sins. If you believe in him and trust in him, he will bring you into his family. He doesn't care where you have been; he cares about where you are going.

Think about the following verses:

> For all have sinned and fall short of the glory of God. (Romans 3:23)

> For by grace you have been saved through faith, and that not of yourselves; *it is* the gift of God, not of works, lest anyone should boast. (Ephesians 2:8–9)

> For God so loved the world that He gave His only begotten Son, that whoever believes in Him should not perish but have everlasting life. (John 3:16)

Consider contacting a local pastor or someone you know who is a Christian. They will be happy to talk with you about their faith and to answer any questions you may have. God loves you!